THIN AIR

MICHELLE PAVER

ISIS
LARGE
PRINT

First published in Great Britain 2016
by
Orion Books
an imprint of The Orion Publishing Group Ltd.

First Isis Edition
published 2017
by arrangement with
Orion Publishing Group Ltd.
An Hachette UK Company
London

A catalogue record for this book is available
from the British Library.

ISBN 978–1–78541–403–9 (hb)
ISBN 978–1–78541–409–1 (pb)

Published by
F. A. Thorpe (Publishing)
Anstey, Leicestershire

Set by Words & Graphics Ltd.
Anstey, Leicestershire
Printed and bound in Great Britain by
T. J. International Ltd., Padstow, Cornwall

This book is printed on acid-free paper

Were we wrong to attempt the conquest of Kangchenjunga? Some would say that we were, and that it is a sin to lay siege to the highest mountains on earth. Moreover, of the three mightiest peaks — Mount Everest, K.2 and Kangchenjunga — seasoned alpinists regard Kangchenjunga as the most lethal. It stands apart from the rest of the Himalaya, its avalanches are legendary, and its rarified air induces a degree of nervous sensibility — one might almost say *abhorrence* — which tests the mettle of the doughtiest man.

Nevertheless, I remain convinced that to vanquish it would be the purest expression of the ideal of Empire: the defeat of the unknown, the triumph of Man over Nature. Yes, our attack on Kangchenjunga failed. Yes, our Expedition ended in tragedy. However, I believe that we who survived may yet hold our heads high, for against terrible odds we retrieved our fallen comrades from the mountain's icy grip, and buried them in a manner befitting Englishmen, having accorded them those honours for which they had so dearly paid.

General Sir Edmund Lyell,
Bloody But Unbowed: the Assault on Mount Kangchenjunga,
1907.

Edmund Lyell is a pompous windbag and third-rate mountaineer who doomed our expedition by fatally underestimating Kangchenjunga. He is also an adroit self-publicist who turned himself into a national hero by penning a "best-selling" account of the tragedy. What his book largely ignores, but what still haunts me decades later, is the fact that although the mountain killed five of our number, we only laid to rest four.

Private memoir of Captain Charles Tennant,
unpublished.

CHAPTER
ONE

Darjeeling, West Bengal, April 1935

"Ah *there* you are, Dr Pearce!" Charles Tennant's daughter comes striding across the lawn with two springer spaniels at her heels. "This dreadful fog, you won't get your view of the mountain now, *what* a shame!"

"Perhaps it'll clear up," I reply, bending to stroke the dogs.

"Heavens no, quite closed in, best come back inside. We can't have the expedition medic catching a chill before you've even set off!"

"Thanks, I shall, directly I finish my cigarette."

"Indeed," she says with a tight little smile.

Millicent Tennant is fortyish and formidable in tweeds, and years of pulling in her lips have sunk creases from mouth to chin, like a ventriloquist's dummy. She seems to enjoy thwarting people, and doesn't approve of me slipping away from her tea party; perhaps she suspects that I'll try to approach her father on the sly. She guards Charles Tennant like a dragon, and clearly relished telling us that because the old man had a "turn" shortly before we arrived, he can't

3

possibly see us, or anyone else, for at least a week. "And by then you'll all have headed off into the wilds, *such* a shame."

The others were wretchedly disappointed, but I don't mind, I'm elated simply to be here. I can't quite believe that after weeks of travelling, I'm standing on a Himalayan ridge seven thousand feet up, in Charles Tennant's rose garden — *Charles Tennant*, the last survivor of the Lyell expedition.

Perhaps it's lack of sleep, but everything around me seems preternaturally intense: the smell of wet roses, the scream of that bird; and from somewhere beyond the mists, the pull of the mountain we're going to climb.

"Do mind the edge, Dr Pearce," warns Millicent Tennant. "Rather a nasty drop."

I lean over the low stone wall, and suck in my breath. "Good Lord, so it is." Through the murk, I can just make out the red glimmer of a native village, horribly far down. The treetops below me are forbiddingly still; but almost within reach, a small, shadowy form stirs on a branch. Perhaps that's one of those macaques about which I've been warned.

I do wish I could see the mountain. I was late reaching Darjeeling, and at the Planters' Club I found an ecstatic note from Kits, summoning me to *tea with Charles Tennant!!* *Who knows, perhaps I shall be the one to persuade him to break his famous silence!!* When I arrived at the old man's bungalow, after a jolting ride in a horse-tonga through misty tea plantations, the others told me what "stupendous

4

views" they'd had only an hour before; but by the time I'd escaped the drawing room and found my way to the garden, clouds had rolled in and the mountain had disappeared.

And they really are *clouds* swirling around me, a dank, silent invasion that's turned the afternoon prematurely dark.

"Did I mention that I know your fiancée's people?" says Millicent Tennant, declining my cigarette case with another tight little smile. "Your ex-fiancée, I should say."

"Really?" I murmur. "I had no idea."

"Oh yes, poor dear Clare is *quite* a favourite. I gather she behaved impeccably. Won't say a word against you." She's watching my face, her small eyes beady with curiosity.

Poor Clare indeed. But I shan't apologise to Millicent Tennant. I did enough apologising in London.

"So frightfully sudden," she remarks. "Scarcely more than a week before the big day."

"I'm afraid it was. But Clare agrees with me that it was for the best." And no, I'm damned if I'll tell you why I broke it off just so that you can tell the whole of Darjeeling. What could I say? That I realised in the nick of time that I was turning into my brother?

The silence lengthens. My hostess's pencilled brows rise. "Well," she says crisply. "The others will be wondering where you are. Your brother, poor fellow, seems rather out of sorts."

The understatement makes me smile. Kits did his best to charm his way into Charles Tennant's presence, and when that failed, he went into a sulk.

"Kits is a little cast down," I explain. "He's revered the Lyell expedition since he was a boy, he can recite whole pages of *Bloody But Unbowed*. He'd set his heart on meeting Captain Tennant."

"Oh, what a shame." She plucks a leaf off her skirt. "Well. I must be getting back to my other guests. Do bear in mind that these are the tropics, Dr Pearce. Darkness falls rather more sharply than what you'll be used to."

"Thank you, I shall."

When at last she's gone, I light another cigarette and let the fog and the smell of wet roses wash her out of my mind.

I lean over the wall. Hard to imagine that down there lies steamy malarial jungle. According to Kits, our mountain's not even fifty miles away, but it'll take us three weeks' hard trekking to get there.

My stomach tightens with excitement. You've done it, Stephen, you've actually done it. No more London, no more Clare, no more apologising. Nothing but snow, ice and rock. A million miles from the messy tangle of human emotions.

It's strange, but since my ship left Southampton, I've scarcely allowed myself to think of the mountain itself; perhaps I was afraid of jinxing things. I've simply pictured a generic white peak, like the Crystal Mountain in that storybook when we were boys.

But now, quite suddenly, it's *real*. I don't care that I can't see it. It sent these clouds, it's making its presence felt. I can feel its cold, clammy breath on my skin.

We set off in three days. I can't wait.

She was right: night has fallen as fast as a door slamming shut.

As I'm stumbling back across the lawn, the darkness moves behind me. Then a head peers over the wall, and a shadowy form slinks off. The macaques are taking over the garden.

I make for the light spilling from the French windows on to the verandah, but at the foot of the steps, I bark my shins on a pile of rocks, and swear.

"Who's there!" calls a man's voice: sharp, well-bred, old.

Oh Lord, these aren't the drawing room doors, I've taken a wrong turn. "I beg your pardon, I've — "

"Don't stand out there like an idiot, come in and shut that bloody door behind you!"

I find myself in a large, dingy study that reeks of stale cigar smoke. Logs crackling in a grate, a moulting tiger skin on the floor, a lamp with a tasselled shade barely lightening the gloom. Smokers' accoutrements are everywhere: table lighters, humidors, brass ash-stands. Piles of papers on a huge sandalwood desk are held down by Indian curios: a vicious curved dagger, a fearsome wooden mask with bulging eyes; and resting on a mahogany box, some kind of native trumpet, fashioned from what was clearly once a human femur.

The owner of the voice sits hunched in an easy chair in the corner furthest from the light, with a plaid rug over his knees. He is old but looks strong: wide shoulders, springing silver hair, small flinty eyes taking my measure. His raw-boned face is mottled with broken veins, and shockingly altered from the famous photograph in which he stands grinning at the camera beside Edmund Lyell, but that lantern jaw and those dark, triangular brows are unmistakable.

At one stroke I'm a boy again, standing in awe before my hero. "You're Charles Tennant," I blurt out inanely.

"Well *done*," he rasps.

"I'm frightfully sorry, sir, I was trying to find the drawing room — "

"Don't fuss, I can't abide fuss! You're here, so you'll stay!"

My God, it's really him. I step forwards and offer my hand, suppressing an ignoble spurt of glee: poor Kits, he'll be incandescent with envy. "Stephen Pearce, sir, how d'you do?"

"You don't look old enough to be a medic," he growls, ignoring my hand.

I permit myself a slight smile. "I'm thirty-four."

"Wasn't there some problem with the medic?"

"I'm a last-minute replacement, sir, he broke his leg in a motor smash three days before they sailed . . ." I trail off in embarrassment. That's not an easy chair he's in; it's a Bath chair: the self-propelling kind with wooden hand-rims to the wheels. Charles Tennant lost both feet to frostbite.

Smiling grimly at my discomfort, he demands to know why I was swearing on his verandah. I mention the rocks, and he gives a mirthless bark. "It's a grave, didn't you notice? Grandson's fox terrier. Stupid little tyke ran under a tonga. The dog, not the boy."

8

I press my lips together and nod. Then I catch sight of a large framed photograph on the wall behind the desk, and I forget everything.

The sight of it is like music, a deep, strong note thrilling through me. It's utterly different from Everest, or Annapurna, or K.2. No lone triangular summit, but a vast broad-shouldered massif spiked with several chaotic peaks, with one jagged fang just dominating the rest. Kangchenjunga.

No one seems to agree on what the name actually means, but most settle for "The Five Treasures of the Snows". Although what does *that* refer to? The peaks? The five enormous glaciers pouring down its flanks?

It catches at my heart, and I feel that peculiar bite of eagerness and dread which I always get before a climb. We're going to conquer that mountain. We're going to be the first men in the world ever to stand on top.

Tennant squints up at the photograph with narrowed eyes, as if it hurts to look. Then, with an odd, convulsive twitch, he turns away. "The Lepcha call it *Kong Chen*," he mutters. "Means 'Big Stone'. Doesn't stop the damn fools worshipping it."

"Can one see it from here, sir?" I've an idea that the French windows face north, although now of course they're black.

"That photograph was taken from where you're standing," says Tennant with startling bitterness. "One never knows when it will appear." He is clutching his knees. His hands are large and powerful, with ropy blue veins. His knuckles are white with strain.

I wonder how he can bear to have the mountain always before him: a constant reminder of the companions who never returned. I wonder what he sees when he looks at that photograph.

And I'm beginning to wish that the others were here with me, because I feel like a badly prepared schoolboy. I'd planned to read up about Lyell on the voyage out, but the porters lost my book-bag at Southampton, so I've only the haziest recollection of what actually happened: a blizzard, an avalanche, and five men dead.

The old man sits hunched in his Bath chair. He is not at all what I expected. In *Bloody But Unbowed*, Charles Tennant was such *fun*: the awfully good sort whom everyone wanted for their best chum. What turned him into this bitter, twitchy wreck of a man?

I suppose what he went through would be enough for anyone — although by all accounts, it didn't alter Edmund Lyell. He lost a leg and a hand, but he made a success of his life: the book, the lecture tours, the knighthood . . .

Tennant misses nothing. "Shattered your illusions, have I? Not another damn fool who's worshipped us since the nursery?"

"No," I say evenly. "I did till I was nine, but then my older brother took my copy of *Bloody But Unbowed*. He's having tea in your drawing room. He'd give anything to be here, talking to you."

"Is he the idiot who's decided you'll try our route up the south-west face?"

I'm taken aback. "I didn't know that we were."

"What, you don't even know where you're *going*?"

Bloody hell, Kits, you might have told me. "As I said, sir, I'm a last-minute replacement. I . . . expect they chose it because it's the best route."

"It is, but you'll never do it."

"Why not? You nearly did."

He hesitates, and his expression turns guarded. "We would have done it if it hadn't been for Lyell. Don't you believe that penny dreadful of his. He was a bad mountaineer, a dreadful leader — and *vain*. 'Heroes' often are."

He speaks with such hatred that I remind myself that he's in his sixties, and, if his daughter is to be believed, far from well.

"The south-west face, sir," I hazard. "Is there a problem with it?"

" — Problem," he mutters. He darts a glance at the photograph, then recoils with a shudder. Something flickers across his face: something very like fear.

Then it's gone, and he's in command of himself. "What *problem* could there possibly be," he rasps, "on the most dangerous mountain in the world? Know the Himalaya, do you? Climbed here before?"

"No, sir. First time in India."

"Good God in Heaven." He gives me a pitying stare that makes me flush.

I decide to throw caution to the winds and put the question I'm burning to ask. "Why did you never write an account of the climb yourself, sir?"

"What the devil gives you the right to ask me that?" His tone is belligerent, but his glance strays to his desk, and I catch my breath. Can it be that he *has* written something?

"I'm sorry if I was impertinent," I say carefully. "But I'm sure you'll understand why we're all so fearfully curious. It's been nearly thirty years, and you've never spoken of it, or written — "

"Brother climbing with brother?" he raps out. "Get on with him, do you?"

The change of subject is so blatant it's an insult, and it slams the door on further questions.

"We've climbed together for years," I reply coolly.

A disbelieving snort. "What about the others?"

"I only met them today, we came out by different routes — "

"So why'd you want to climb it?"

"I'm sorry?"

"You heard me, why?"

"Does one need a reason?"

Surprisingly, he seems to like that. The corners of his mouth turn down in a grim smile. "You're aware that Norton regards it as harder than Everest?"

"Yes, so I've read."

In the silence that follows, it feels as if the spectres of Norton's ill-fated companions, Mallory and Irvine, are with us in the room.

The silence continues. The old man seems to have forgotten about me. He is still clutching his knees and clenching his lantern jaw. "It'll kill you if it can," he says between his teeth. "Oh yes. You have no idea . . ."

Once more, he glances at the photograph — and recoils with that strange, convulsive shudder.

12

And now I'm sure of it. He's frightened. Charles Tennant, one of the toughest mountaineers who ever lived, is *frightened* of that mountain.

"Hand me that box on the desk," he snaps, making me jump.

"Um — which one, sir?"

"The one with the *kangling* on top."

"I'm sorry, the what?"

"The trumpet, damnit!"

Removing the thigh-bone trumpet from the lid, I do as he says. He places the mahogany box on his knees, then covers it with both hands.

My heart begins to thud. Has he been keeping me here for a reason? Appraising me? Nerving himself to tell me — *what*?

Or am I letting fatigue and excitement distort my judgement?

The silence has become intolerable, and he shows no sign of breaking it.

I'm still holding the thigh-bone trumpet. Its mouthpiece is blackened silver, its other end studded with grimy turquoise. For something to say, I ask him what it sounds like.

His head swings round, and he stares up at me with undisguised horror. "*What?*" he says in a cracked voice. "What it — *sounds* like? What the devil d'you mean by that?"

Christ, what have I said? The blood is draining from his face, and his lips are turning grey. My idle question seems to have tipped him over the edge.

He's rocking back and forth, and his gaze has turned inwards, into the past. "*Every night*," he whispers. "*Every* night, do you understand, I see them . . . my comrades of Kangchenjunga. I see their arms outstretched . . . I hear their cries for help . . . Yes . . . I shall always see them . . ."

I'm casting about for water, Scotch, anything. Decanter on a bookshelf: brandy by the smell. I splash some in a tumbler and hold it to his lips, but he thrusts me aside with startling strength.

"Get out!" he shouts. "Get out, and don't come back!"

CHAPTER
TWO

Kits is seething as we share a horse-tonga back to Darjeeling.

"What were you *doing*, blundering in on Captain Tennant? And why the *hell* didn't you fetch me?"

"He wouldn't have let me," I reply. "He's rather — imperious."

"Well I wouldn't know, would I, since I've never met him, and I'm hardly likely to now! Christ, Stephen, what did you *say* to him?"

"Nothing. He worked himself into a state, talking about the past. Why didn't you tell me we'll be following Lyell's route?"

"I'd have thought you'd have gathered that by now!"

How? I want to retort. We only saw each other once before he left for Bombay. I was having a dreadful time with Clare's people, and he was in a fix because he needed a medic. The question of routes never came up.

We're sitting side by side in the tonga, facing backwards. Kits is staring rigidly at the road. His eyes are glassy with rage, and the corners of his mouth are pulled down, like a bulldog's. He used to do that when we were boys, and he was about to beat me up.

I'm tempted to tell him that Old Man Tennant thinks he's an idiot for choosing the south-west face; but I've promised myself we won't fight. Hang it all, we're grown men.

The road is a dark, receding tunnel of dripping deodars and creaking bamboo. The rain has held off, but it's cold, and around us the clouds are dense and ceaselessly moving: a visitation from another world.

I feel shaken and guilty about the old man, although for the life of me, I can't think why an idle question about some grubby native curio should have tipped him over the edge.

I keep seeing Millicent Tennant administering his "drops", and despatching me with a basilisk stare that declared my medical expertise very much *de trop*. I keep seeing the terror in the old man's eyes.

I find that terror profoundly shocking. The idea that a white man — a sahib — should be frightened of a mountain.

Of course, for any climber, there's always an element of fear. Fear, desire, awe, respect, even love. But not fear to the exclusion of all else. And Tennant wasn't deranged. I'm sure of that. So *why*?

There's something else, too. I've a nagging suspicion that he *has* written some kind of account of the expedition.

Well, that settles it. I shan't say a word of this to Kits. God knows what he'd do if he found out that I've blown our chances of getting hold of it.

"So why *are* we following Lyell?" I ask. "I can't say I like the idea, we'll be constantly reminded of disaster."

"Why must you always *analyse*? I hope you're not going to go in for that on the expedition, the other chaps won't like it at all!"

"Noted. So why follow Lyell?"

"Because it's the best route!"

"Is that all there is to it?"

"What d'you mean?"

"Oh, I don't know," I say drily. "Following your hero's footsteps, finishing what he began . . ."

"Yes, go on, mock. It's what you do best, isn't it?"

I hold up my hands.

But I know my brother. A couple of years ago, someone came upon Irvine's ice-axe on Everest's north-west ridge, and Kits sulked for weeks. Why wasn't *he* the one to find it and get the glory? That's what he's after now: relics of the Lyell expedition; and a chance to complete what the great man began, by being the first in the world to conquer an eight-thousand-metre peak — with the added lustre of planting the Union Jack on the summit, and beating the bloody Germans.

I wish I hadn't let the old man unsettle me. Still, I suppose it's a lesson. I must remember that whatever happened to him was nearly thirty years ago. I mustn't let his fear taint my mountain. I mustn't let it infect me.

So in a way, losing my books was a stroke of luck. And I'm damned if I'll borrow any of Kits'. I shan't read a word about the Lyell expedition, I don't want to know what happened to them. It's in the past. *It has nothing to do with us.*

I catch a smell of charcoal and manure, and a distant clamour of dogs: we're approaching Darjeeling.

Without turning my head, I say, "I hear there's rather a jolly bazaar. Have you been?"

Kits snorts. "Usual native rubbish. I picked up a few trinkets that'll amuse Dorothy and the boys."

"How are they?"

"Harry's homesick, but he'll get over it. Ronnie'll soon be Captain of the First Eleven." His lip curls. "Chip off the old block. Dorothy's run off her feet, of course. Village fête, and so on. Busy time on the estate."

"Yes, of course."

Crows fly up with a clatter of wings from something small and dead at the side of the road.

I say to Kits: "I think Clare's father is going to sue me for breach of promise."

He flicks me an irritable glance, then goes back to scowling at the road.

He always does this. Either we talk about him and his family, or climbing, or we don't talk at all.

"Did Captain Tennant say anything else about the route?" he says.

I hesitate. "Only that he doesn't think we'll do it."

He turns his head. "Why ever not?"

"I asked, but he wouldn't say."

In places, the whitewashed stones marking the roadside are spattered with dark-red blotches that look like blood. I ask Kits what they are and he says it's *pan*. At my blank expression, he rolls his eyes. "Betel juice! The natives chew it, then spit it out. Good Lord, Stephen, what were you *doing* all those weeks on the

18

ship? I threw you a lifeline when I asked you to come, don't you forget it! I'd have thought the least you could do would be to familiarise yourself with where you're bloody well going!"

"I meant to, but the porters lost my books."

"Christ, that is so like you!"

I turn to him. "Kits. *Pax*."

He stares moodily ahead, then cuffs me hard on the ear. "Sometimes, little brother, you are the absolute *end!*"

Astonishing what a good dinner and a few whiskies and soda can do for a man. My unease about Charles Tennant has quite worn off, and I've smoothed Kits' ruffled feathers by asking him all about his new billiard room, and how young Ronnie acquitted himself on his first hunt.

We've settled ourselves in the smoking room of the Planters' Club, and are awaiting our leader, Major Cotterell, who has convened a "council of war". None of us has an earthly what it's about.

We've drawn our easy chairs close to the fire, and behind us, large palms in brass pots lend a pleasing air of privacy. As I survey my fellow sahibs through a haze of cigar smoke, I feel less like the new boy at school.

McLellan is a plump young Scot with carroty hair and freckles; I'll have to keep an eye on him for sunburn. He's on extended leave from a regiment in the Punjab, and strikes me as the officious type, so he's well suited to being in charge of porters and supplies. He's fluent in Nepalese and what he calls "bazaar

Hindi", and is the only one of us who's done any climbing in the Himalaya. He's also a shade off in the vowels, and seems very eager to fit in.

I know Garrard slightly from Winchester, where he was Kits' best friend. He'll be handling communications: press despatches, photography and weather reports wirelessed from Darjeeling. An atheist, a snob and a parlour Socialist, he's flamboyantly ugly, with thinning fair hair, brown-ringed eyes set too close together, and an enormous hooked nose. Although clever and bookish, he's always been devoted to Kits; it's one of those ill-assorted friendships that simply works. Over dinner, I asked him why he had joined the expedition, and he flushed. "Why, because Kits asked. Simple as that."

At Winchester, everyone called him "Beak", for obvious reasons, but the three of us have agreed to dispense with nicknames, so as not to exclude the others. Thus Garrard will be Garrard, and I'm no longer "Bodge". Thank God. I've hated that ever since Kits made it up on my first day at school.

Kits, of course, remains Kits. No one's called him Christopher since he was born. As our best gun, he'll provide us with game on the trek to the mountain; and since he's also our finest climber, he'll give us our best shot at the summit.

Major Cotterell strides in, and we spring to our feet. He motions us down, then takes up position on the rug in front of the fire.

"Matter of some delicacy," he says, frowning as he crams tobacco in his briar pipe. "I've had a note from

Captain Tennant, urging us in the strongest terms not to follow their route up the south-west face."

There's a stunned silence.

I surprise myself by speaking first. "I'm aware that I don't know as much as the rest of you, but . . . if we tackled the north face instead, wouldn't that mean an entirely different route, even to get there?"

"Well of course it would!" barks McLellan in a tone that makes me blink. "I'd have to find whole new teams of coolies and yak-wallahs, it's simply not on!"

"Why ever does he *want* us to alter our plans?" says Garrard, pulling his great beak in a gesture I remember from school.

"He doesn't say" Cotterell turns to me. "Did he mention anything to you, Dr Pearce?"

"Only that he didn't think we'd succeed, sir; not that we shouldn't try."

"Is it possible that he's right?" muses Garrard. "I mean, until now, most chaps have attempted the north face — "

"How can you *say* that?" explodes Kits. "We've been over this a million times, Lyell's is the best route!"

Garrard flicks him an apologetic glance. "Kits, I was merely wondering. Smythe preferred the north face. And there are those who say that the south-west is unclimbable."

"*Who* says?" retorts Kits.

"Well, Bauer."

"He's *German*," sneers Kits. "This is our chance to see that an Englishman's first to the top!"

"Hear, hear," says Cotterell. He's the only one of us old enough to have fought in the War. I'd imagine that for him, beating the Hun is personal.

"They say Bauer's planning to give it another shot next year," adds Kits. "Wouldn't you love to be there, sir, when he learns that we've pipped him to the post?"

Cotterell chuckles. "And yet, my boy . . . Perhaps Captain Tennant is warning us off because he knows from bitter experience that the south-west face can't be done."

"Oh, sir — "

"Or perhaps," the Major goes on, "and I know this sounds the most fearful rot, but *perhaps* he feels that that route sort of — 'belongs' to Lyell? Oughtn't we at least to consider respecting his wishes?"

McLellan's freckled face goes pink. "Really, sir, I can't see why we're even discussing this, there isn't *time*! In seven weeks the Monsoon will turn that mountain into a deathtrap — "

"You mean, more of a deathtrap," grins Garrard.

The Scotsman ignores that. "We have to be off it by the end of May, sir, we *can't* go in for last-minute changes!"

This seems unanswerable to me. I'm curious to see what Major Cotterell will decide.

He is every boy's ideal of a mountaineer: tall, well-built, with a handsome leonine head silvering at the temples, and grey eyes that a certain type of journalist would call "piercing". At well over forty, he's the oldest of us by several years, and his military experience makes him admirably suited to the role of expedition leader. But there's a band of flaky skin at his hairline, and I wonder if he's a worrier.

"Well," he says, stroking his moustache. "I want this to be a democratic venture, so I shall call for a show of hands."

Before I know what's happened, he and Garrard have voted in favour of changing the route, Kits and McLellan against, and everyone's looking at me. *Hell*, I've got the casting vote.

Logs hiss in the hearth, and outside, some night bird utters an alien shriek. If I believed in omens, I'd say it was warning us against following Lyell. Omens or not, I hate the idea. We'd be climbing in dead men's footsteps.

However. Kits is glowering at me. I'm only too aware that behind his stolid, *Just William* features, there's a streak of ruthlessness a mile wide. *You're here because of me, little brother, so you'd bloody well better back me up.*

There's something else, too. Something that has nothing to do with Kits. Charles Tennant didn't think we could do this. I want to prove him wrong.

"Come on, Stephen," says Kits between his teeth. "What's it to be?"

It's so quiet, you can almost hear the smoke rise.

I think of that photograph in Tennant's study: Kangchenjunga, floating in majesty above the clouds.

"I don't see that we have a choice," I say at last. "It's either the south-west face, or we scratch the whole show. So let's stick to our guns. The south-west face it is."

CHAPTER
THREE

I know that I'm dreaming, but it doesn't help. I'm holding the snow globe. I've just shaken it, and the blizzard is smothering the tiny cottage and the miniature man in the porch.

I am that man. I am trapped in the white silence — and yet I see myself from outside. Snow up to my thighs, thick flakes clogging eyes and nose and mouth. Now my face is beginning to change. I'm turning into Kits . . .

I wake with a jolt. I burrow into my pillow with a groan.

I am so *sick* of that bloody dream. Every night for two months. You'd have thought my unconscious mind could come up with something a little less thumpingly obvious. "Snow globe" equals "trapped in a life I don't want". And that transformation into Kits . . . I understand, now can we stop?

Things had been going swimmingly in London: plum job in Harley Street, girlfriend the senior partner's daughter. Then within a week, I found myself engaged, and Clare's papa was offering me a junior partnership. I had a nagging feeling that something was wrong, but I couldn't work out what.

The snow globe was a wedding present. "Isn't he *darling*?" cried Clare, burying the little man in snow.

That night, I had the dream for the first time. I knew at once what it meant. If I married Clare, I'd end up like Kits. Kits with his well-heeled existence, his impeccably connected wife, and his bouncing progeny. I had thought I wanted all that, but now I felt breathless and trapped. I had to break out of the snow globe before it was too late.

The next day, Clare's grandmamma gave a dinner. I told my poor fiancée over the soup. She wasn't so much hurt as indignant, and not entirely surprised. Then I told her papa. Then I stood up and told everyone else. All my pretty chickens at one fell swoop. Aunt Ruth always said I was given to extremes.

Kits has never asked me why I did it, and so far, Cotterell and McLellan have also steered clear. But last night before dinner, Garrard did, so I told him.

"I was in danger of becoming a younger version of Kits," I explained.

"Would that be so bad?" he said quietly.

"Oh, you know what I mean."

He stroked his beak like a thoughtful vulture. "But then — why climb with him?"

I blinked. "Well. That's different. I want to climb the mountain. It doesn't belong to Kits."

His close-set eyes twinkled. "And anything he can do . . ."

I snorted a laugh. "It's not like that! This is the chance of a lifetime! This is Kangchenjunga!"

It's still dark, and the native dogs are barking fit to wake the dead. Now I know why they sleep all day: it's because they bark all night. The luminous dials of my wrist watch tell me it's four o'clock. In two hours, we set off.

My stomach is churning. I've never been on an expedition. Most of my climbs have been in the Alps: up and down in a day, then back to the hotel for a bath. I do hope I measure up.

Shivering, I check my gear for the umpteenth time. Kitbag, bedding roll, beloved Swiss climbing boots, trusty Norwegian rucksack, japanned tin medicine case; thank *God* I put my medical papers in that, and not the book-bag.

I know what's rattled me. It's not the dream, it's the coolies' wretched superstitions. The day before yesterday, they got wind that we'll be following Lyell's route, and it scared them rigid. I've no idea why, but there was quite a row.

It was an overcast morning (still no mountain), and they were waiting on some flattish ground at the edge of town.

I hadn't expected that there'd be so many of them. "You told me this was a small show," I said to Kits. "Why do we need *sixty* porters?"

He shrugged. "That's small for the Himalayas. Dyhrenfurth and Smythe had more than four hundred."

I was surprised to see several older men among them, and even some women. All were small, slight people with high-boned faces burnished by wind and sun, *pan*-stained teeth, and frightened expressions. Most sported earrings of turquoise or coral, and grimy silver amulets on their breasts. A few wore European clothes (I gather that's a sign of rank), but the rest were in colourful calf-length robes that left their scrawny shins naked.

I was concerned that the majority were barefoot, and I queried this with McLellan. He said he'd be issuing boots in Nepal, once the "laggards" had dropped out; he seemed offended that I'd asked. I'm afraid he might be a bit of a martinet. I hope that's not going to be a problem.

The row erupted as I was heading for the tin-roofed shack where I'd set up my "clinic". Cotterell was standing beside a mountain of big wooden packing crates, chatting to the Assistant DC and a fellow from the Himalayan Club. McLellan was seated on a camp stool under a tree. He wore a white pith helmet on his carroty head, and he seemed to be enjoying himself, taking names and thumbprints in receipt for pay and rations, which were being dispensed by Garrard and Kits.

Suddenly, the Scotsman leapt to his feet and started ranting in some unintelligible tongue at two natives who stood before him with respectfully averted eyes.

It turned out they were the *sirdar* — the headman — and his assistant, and they were flatly refusing to set off the next day as planned, because that happened to be the same day on which Lyell had set off in '06.

"Or so they *say*," fumed McLellan, who'd gone puce beneath his freckles. "It's a filthy trick to extort more rations!"

"Can't we just let them wait another day?" I asked.

He stared at me. "Give in to a coolie once, Dr Pearce, and there'll be no end to his tricks!"

"But why do they *mind* the date?" said Kits. "I rather like the idea of leaving on the same day as Lyell."

"The plan," snapped McLellan, "is for the coolies to leave tomorrow on foot, with us catching up the next day by motor — and that's what we'll do."

He launched into another tirade at the two natives, and things looked grim. Then the tirade became more measured. Finally, the natives broke into grins.

"I'm sending a runner with their hats," muttered McLellan. "It's preposterous, but provided their *hats* leave today, they'll feel they've made a start. Bad karma averted, and all that rot."

"Clever," I remarked.

He gave me a cool look. "I do know these people, Dr Pearce. The coolie is half child, half devil, and an inveterate liar. You'd do well to remember that."

"How do we reassure them about following Lyell's route?" said Garrard, scratching his untidy fair hair.

"We don't," said the Scotsman. "They'll forget; they're easily distracted."

"Hope you're right, old chap," murmured Garrard.

I left them to it, and went to begin my medical checks.

My clinic was full, and I found myself in an oniony fug of unwashed flesh. McLellan had tartly reminded me to "worm the coolies", and my predecessor, poor Hewet, had laid in supplies for mass inoculations against smallpox, typhoid and typhus. To a man (and woman), the coolies politely accepted my doses of santonin and castor oil — and just as politely declined to be inoculated.

In desperation, I rolled up my sleeve and inoculated myself. Still no good. I was beginning to despair when one of them stepped forwards and offered himself for sacrifice.

He looked about fifty, a small, squat goblin with a wrinkled mahogany face, and teeth and lips stained purple with *pan*. He wore a green robe criss-crossed across the chest, a knitted yellow cap with a scarlet bobble on top, and a black pigtail down his back. Thrust in his belt was a reed flute and a vicious curved dagger, like the one on Charles Tennant's desk (all the natives have them). In heavily accented English, he told me his name was Nima. Then, with a big purple grin, he bared his powerful arm.

After I'd inoculated him, the others swiftly fell into line, laughing and joshing as they submitted to the needle. McLellan calls them all coolies — I don't know if that's a collective term or a job description — but I could see there were different races, and I had Nima point them out. Bhutia, Lepcha, Limbu, Sherpa. Nima's a Sherpa. He told me proudly that Sherpas are from Nepal, and they're much the best climbers. He seems to look down on the others.

I wish I knew more about them, and I wonder if McLellan's view of them can be right. Once their fears over Lyell were laid to rest, they seemed rather happy people to me, friendly, and with a lively sense of fun.

If only they weren't so confoundedly superstitious. Most wore narrow white ribbon-like scarves painted with fine black squiggles, and when I asked Nima, he gave me another purple grin. "Prayers, Doctor Sahib."

"To whom?"

His grin wavered. "They are keeping away bad things."

"Bad things?"

" — In the mountains, Doctor Sahib."

The depth of my dismay startled me. I felt slightly sick. *Why?* It's not as if I believe in this tosh. I'm a doctor. And like Garrard, I've no faith in "higher powers".

The dogs are still barking. It's a red dawn, the first day of our expedition, but Darjeeling remains shrouded in cloud. I wonder if Nima thinks that's good or bad.

Ours will be a small, fast expedition: twelve Sherpas and fifty lowland coolies — unlike those vast, bloated Everest affairs. Major Cotterell has planned the whole show with military precision, and last night, we went over our route. North through the jungles of the Sikkimese foothills, west over the great Singalila Ridge (some sixteen thousand feet high), then down into Nepal, and up the Yalung Glacier to the mountain's south-west face. For the first four nights we'll be sleeping in dak-bungalows — I gather they're government rest-houses — and after that, tents.

As for the mountain itself, Kits warned me in London not to get my hopes up about making the team for the summit, and he repeated that last night. I didn't care for being put in my place in front of the others, but

I don't really mind about the summit, I only want to climb. I just hope I don't let them down.

I suppose I still feel a bit of an outsider. Kits, Garrard and Cotterell travelled out together, and McLellan knows the country and the natives. All I have is my medical expertise: what Kits calls "high-brow stuff". It doesn't really help.

But I do love the sound of that glacier. I'm longing for glittering pinnacles of ice, and deep blue crevasses. A simpler world, far away from Harley Street and snow globes.

And I think I know why I've conceived such a dislike of the coolies' superstitions. They remind me of Charles Tennant. I see him now, crouching in his study among those ghastly curios: that glaring mask and that thigh-bone trumpet. The coolies are scared of the mountain, and so is he. That's what I can't bear. I want it clean and unsullied.

McLellan's trick with the hats was clever, but unwise. By humouring the coolies' beliefs, he's given undue importance to Lyell — and that's something we *must* avoid. An expedition that took place twenty-nine years ago *can't* have anything to do with ours. It cannot possibly affect us, unless we let it.

This is *much* better. Already, Darjeeling feels a million miles away.

We left after breakfast in three Austin motor cars driven by a trio of breezy young English tea planters who'd agreed to "run us down to Singla Bazaar" — "us" being the five sahibs, the cook, Pasang (the handsome young assistant *sirdar*), and two other Sherpas, who'll see to our needs until we catch up with the rest of the coolies tonight, at the first dak-bungalow.

A cuckoo sounded an incongruous note as we wound our way down through the wet green hills, and I glimpsed tea terraces when the mist allowed — which mostly it didn't.

"Such a shame," remarked the chap at the wheel. "The views are stupendous." I'm becoming rather tired of hearing that.

Now it's noon, the motors have gone, and we've picked up our ponies. Mine is a scrawny little grey with a drooping feather in his browband. I can't pronounce his name, so I call him Flick, as he enjoys swishing his tail in my face.

My saddle is hideously uncomfortable, but I don't care. We're in the jungle. The air is alive with mosquitoes and the shrieks of unseen birds. There's a rank smell of decay, and it's *hot*. My bush shirt is soaking wet, and I've reminded everyone to wear their hats and take their quinine.

Before us glides a jade-green river, spanned by a rickety native suspension bridge, cobbled together from frayed rope and very dodgy-looking planks. Once we're across, we'll be in Sikkim, and the expedition will truly have begun.

The bridge is festooned with hundreds of small, rather jolly flags coloured blue, white, red, green and yellow.

"Apparently," says Garrard with his formidable nose in a book. "*Each flag is inscribed with Buddhist prayers*

32

which are released at every gust, in a lazy but ingenious ruse to avoid effort."

My heart sinks. The book is *Bloody But Unbowed*. I wonder if we're to be treated to excerpts at every step.

Between us and the bridge stands what looks like a large stone urn; this too is sacred. Garrard calls it a *chorten*. As I plod past it on Flick, a Sherpa darts out, respectfully takes hold of my bridle, and tries to lead us around the other side.

It's Nima, the one who volunteered to be inoculated. "Always left, Doctor Sahib," he says with a shy smile. "Left, like the sun."

Our old nurse used to insist on the same thing with churches: always clockwise, never widdershins. But I can't allow this sort of unreason, so I tell Nima firmly, "Thank you, but I shall go on the right, as I intended."

With a bow he stands back, and watches me pass on the "wrong" side, with something like pity on his brown goblin face; as if I'm a puppy in danger of walking off a cliff.

"Did you know," says Garrard, still reading, "there's a god on Kangchenjunga? And this river is fed by its glaciers."

"Is that why they're making offerings?" says Kits.

Each of the coolies is tossing in a few grains from the twisted strip of cloth that holds his rations.

"Well, my cigarette stub will have to do," yawns Garrard, flicking it in as he leads his pony across.

"It'll get nothing from me," says McLellan, who's a staunch Presbyterian.

"Or me," I mutter with feeling.

The bridge sways alarmingly as I lead Flick on, but he takes it in his stride, and we soon reach the other side.

To my irritation, Kits has tossed in a handful of annas.

"Why on earth did you do that?" I exclaim.

"Why on earth not? A few pennies to mark the occasion! After all, Lyell came this way twenty-nine years ago *to the day*."

"But Kits, not in front of the natives!"

"Dr Pearce is right," Cotterell says quietly. "Unwise to sink to their level, Kits old chap. Best to maintain the proper distance."

Kits flushes. "Sorry, sir, won't happen again." When the Major's back is turned, he shoots me a dirty look.

The stupid thing is, he's botched his wretched offering. Some of his coins didn't reach the river, they've landed on the bridge.

A couple of macaques stream down a tree trunk and sidle over to pick them up; but Kits has ridden ahead and doesn't see.

CHAPTER
FOUR

It's just as well that Flick is sure-footed, because there's a lethal drop to the river, and the trail's nothing but mud.

The rain began soon after we crossed into Sikkim. Hot, thunderous, tropical rain. We've been riding for hours, toiling up one steep forested spur, slithering down the other side, wobbling across yet another rickety bridge, then up the next spur, to start all over again.

I wouldn't mind if it weren't for the leeches: tiny evil black worms inching towards us and dangling from every leaf. I've been attacked on my knees, wrists and once, to my horror, my neck. I kill the disgusting little brutes with a burning cigarette, but our barefoot coolies pinch them off without breaking step. My poor pony is suffering; I have to keep jumping down to check his fetlocks and ears. And it helps not a jot that Kits says Lyell never even *saw* a leech, as the weather on his trek was "glorious" all the way.

Kits is riding ahead with the faithful Garrard at his side, while McLellan, his freckled face puce beneath his topi, is keeping close to Major Cotterell. This means I'm on my own, but that's fine as I don't have to chat.

I'm finding the jungle rather oppressive. This steamy smell of decay. These birds one hardly ever sees — and when one does, they're utterly bizarre. Earlier, a magpie flashed past, but it was *blue*, with a yellow-striped tail a yard long.

The trees are even worse. Every trunk, every twisted branch and tangled root is dripping with creepers and moss. All this rank disorder. It's like a forest in a dream.

Even familiar plants are *unfamiliar*. The leaves of the nettles are covered in virulent green blisters; and can that gigantic tree with the throbbing red blossoms be a *rhododendron*? Cotterell, a keen amateur botanist, keeps exclaiming at the magnolias and waxy white orchids. Just now, he called me over to admire a giant "flower", its trumpet-shaped head a blotched greenish-purple, and bowed, like a cobra about to strike. He says it's a snake lily. I think it's revolting.

The rain is easing off at last, and we've come across three lads waiting for us under a tree. They look about ten, with shaven scalps and scarlet robes, but apparently they're Buddhist monks, and they want to take us to their monastery for a blessing — or to beg the mountain not to kill us, I'm unsure which.

We're all eager to reach our billet for the night, but surprisingly, Cotterell thinks we ought to go with them: "Courtesy to the Maharajah, that sort of thing." It turns out that we needed the Maharajah's permission to climb the mountain, and he only gave it on condition that we swore not to stand on the very top, lest we offend the spirit, or god, or whatever it is that haunts the summit.

36

I wish Cotterell hadn't agreed. Are we to be pursued by superstition even on the climb? Surely he can see that by humouring these beliefs — this fear of the mountain — we risk being infected ourselves?

Still, at least the monastery isn't far. It's decrepit, yet strangely impressive: dim, cold spaces hazed with incense and lit by small butter lamps of gleaming bronze. Our coolies leave their packs outside and prostrate themselves, touching their foreheads to the floor. Their belief is extraordinarily strong. I wish I didn't find it so unsettling.

We sahibs take our seats on stools in a muddy courtyard, and wait for whatever-it-is to begin. Nima quietly tells me it's meant to show us the right path after death, but McLellan calls it a "devil dance"; being a Presbyterian, he regards spirits as utterly beyond the pale. Either way, it's hardly reassuring.

The chanting begins: tuneless and surging, like a river. A monk strikes a green drum with a sinuous brass hammer. Another blows an enormously long horn in a deep, other-worldly drone that evokes the echoing boom of mountains.

Now the "devils" leap out. Shaggy dead-grass wigs and flying robes, rattling with tiny bones that I'm pretty sure are human metatarsals. Most of the "devils" wear white skull masks with great ghoulish black eyes, but one of them seems to be a god. His mask is painted a lifeless blue-grey, with yellow fangs and glaring red eyes that remind me unpleasantly of the mask in Tennant's study. Bloody Tennant. Why think of him now?

Faster and faster the devils whirl, stamping their bare feet in an insistent rhythm that thuds right through me.

All of a sudden, the "god" leaps towards me and thrusts his mask in my face. I jerk back with a cry. For an instant, from those painted sockets, I could have sworn that Charles Tennant's flinty eyes glared out at me.

The dancers are whirling away, but my heart is pounding, and my fellow sahibs are staring.

McLellan barks a laugh. "Good Lord, Dr Pearce! Not letting this mumbo jumbo put you in a funk?"

"'Course not," I snap. My cheeks are burning. What must they *think*?

The light is dying by the time we reach our first dak-bungalow. It's at about five thousand feet, on a wooded ridge above a straggling native village. The *chaukidar*, or caretaker, is a villainous old opium addict with yellow eyes. The bungalow is reserved for us sahibs. The coolies have built themselves shelters from branches and bamboo.

It turns out that Nima is my personal servant; each sahib has one. In no time, he's unpacked my gear, brought a basin of hot water, and bustled off to see to Flick.

Of the three beds in the larger room, he's nabbed the best for me: a simple kindness that steadies me a lot. Not that I need steadying, but I'm annoyed with myself for having taken fright at that mask.

We dine on the verandah, on tough grey meat and stewed greens, tinned pears and condensed milk. If it wasn't for the lashings of Scotch, we might be at school. It's raining again. The noise on the tin roof is deafening, but that doesn't prevent the others from ribbing me about what Kits delights in calling "my fainting fit". I don't mind; only McLellan doesn't know when to stop. In the end, I say my goodnights and take myself off.

The downpour is over, and the night is alive with secret tricklings.

I hadn't noticed till now, but this bungalow is really rather dreadful. Green walls oozing damp. A pervasive smell of mouldy canvas. The jungle thrusting in through broken shutters.

My bed is a flimsy native *charpoy* sprung with strips of knotted cloth, and Nima has draped my mosquito net over four bamboo poles tied to the legs. As I shake out my sleeping bag, something drops to the floor and scuttles past my foot. A scorpion. I crush it under my boot.

Somehow, turning in has lost its appeal, so I wander outside for a last cigarette.

The red fires of the coolies flicker in the dark. Nima sits near one, cradling a bowl of *tsampa*, the natives' barley gruel. He has the inward look of a man at prayer, and before starting his meal, he flicks a gobbet at the shadows.

Christ, what a way to live. Must he make an offering before every meal? How can he *imagine* it'll do any good?

On a nearby boulder, someone has placed the head of a goat; presumably that's the remains of our dinner. In the gloom, I make out the brute's thick grey tongue protruding between its teeth. Its half-open eye watches me slyly. Beside it, someone has placed a snake lily and a bunch of those funereal white orchids. Not another bloody offering.

Suddenly, I've had enough. "*Nima!*" I roar. "Come here at once and take this disgusting thing away!"

Leaping to his feet, he scurries to obey.

Behind him, the tip of a cigar glimmers, and Cotterell strolls over. "Trouble, Dr Pearce?"

"Not any more," I say crisply. I'm dismayed to find that my heart is racing. My hands tremble as I light another cigarette.

Cotterell grimaces as he watches Nima bear the thing away. "Offering to the mountain, I'd imagine," he murmurs. "Poor devils blame it for everything: storms, floods, earthquakes. I gather that in the past, it wasn't only goats. Sure you're all right?"

"Fine. Really."

He strokes his moustache, then clears his throat. "McLellan rather overdid the joshing at dinner, but you mustn't mind him. He's not exactly Varsity, and he feels it. But he's a sound officer and a good man."

Cotterell's on the wrong track, but I'm glad he's changed the subject. I ask him why McLellan joined the expedition.

"He's a son of the manse," he says, inclining his leonine head. "Grew up in some parish in Glasgow, father's still a minister there. Tells me he reads his bible every night. Seems to feel that climbing gets him closer to, um, God."

"Ah. And you, sir? Beating the Hun, and all that?"

He chuckles. "Well, someone's got to stop them! They're after revenge because they lost the War. But we can't go on letting them get away with it, or why did we fight? First it was the Eiger. Now *this* mountain. They've tackled it three times, so they think it's theirs!"

"Like us with Everest?"

He laughs. "*Touché,* Dr Pearce! And you? Kits tells me you used to do a good deal of climbing."

"We were brought up by an aunt with a fondness for doomed heroes. Whymper and the Matterhorn, that sort of thing. She was a pretty decent climber herself, so we spent every holiday in the Alps."

"And yet only Kits has kept it up."

"Small matter of having to earn my living, sir."

"Ah yes, of course. So in a way — Kits has been climbing for you both?"

No, I'm tempted to reply, Kits climbs for himself, because he's the oldest and inherited a fortune and married money.

"You know," says Cotterell, "I've read about the Himalaya all my life. Had a copy of Freshfield in the trenches." He scratches his hairline. "I was fifteen when Lyell set off. Kept a map on my wall. Used to mark his position with pins."

"I did the same for Captain Scott."

"Ah yes, you'd have been too young for Lyell."

I smile. "I wasn't quite five."

We smoke in silence.

I like Cotterell. He strikes me as a romantic — which is odd, given his time in the trenches; although that seems to have left him curiously unmarked. I fancy he's

41

not so different from the schoolboy who tracked his hero's progress on a map.

"Kits tells me you lost your books," he says. "I have Freshfield, Smythe — Lyell, of course. Happy to lend them whenever you wish."

I'm unprepared for the strength of my response. The idea fills me with visceral revulsion. "That's awfully kind of you, sir," I say, struggling to keep my voice steady, "but I don't think that's wise. In fact — if you'll forgive me, I think it's distinctly unhealthy. We need to concentrate on the task ahead. We can't let ourselves be distracted by disasters from the past. Especially not Lyell."

He draws on his cigar, then nods. "Sound. Very sound. Thank you, Dr Pearce. I'll spread the word." He bids me goodnight and strolls inside.

Soon afterwards, I follow. A thorough search with my electric torch reveals no more scorpions, and I wriggle into my sleeping bag.

I'm exhausted, but wide awake. The jungle, the devil dance, that goat's head on the rock . . . And *Lyell*. I can't bear the thought of following in dead men's footsteps. I can't bear the idea of being infected by Charles Tennant's irrational fear.

Thank God I talked to Cotterell. Thank God there's to be no more Lyell.

CHAPTER
FIVE

Seven days out, and this weather's getting on my nerves. I can feel the mountains in the thinness of the air, but I still haven't seen them.

We're at their mercy, though. So far, they've sent sleet, hail, rain and snow; sometimes the whole lot within an hour. The change comes without warning. It plays with one's perceptions. It's making me jumpy.

Right now, it's freezing fog, and two Sherpas have gone ahead to mark the way with cairns. They call them "stone men". None of us likes the way they loom out of the mist. Maybe that's why the coolies are making trouble again about following Lyell's route. It's taken ages to settle them.

We left the ponies at the last village. As we trudged higher, we emerged from the jungle and hacked our way through tortured thickets of dwarf rhododendron, and out on to bleak, stony uplands. I can't shake a sense of unreality. The fairy-tale forests are far below, and we've emerged into this eerie upper world haunted by unseen creatures: snow leopard, wild blue sheep — and the coolies' imaginary spirits.

To them, this wilderness is thronged. Every rock and stream possesses its own demon. They refuse to burn rubbish, for fear of the fire spirits, and rarely venture out after dark.

Even we white men are finding the sheer *immensity* hard to take. Like ants, we pick our way around gigantic boulders, and over thunderous torrents whose roars follow us up deserted valleys. We all feel our insignificance. We keep it at bay with routine.

Nima wakes me at five with tea, while the coolies flit about like wraiths, striking camp. We march for two hours, then halt for breakfast: bacon, eggs and *chuppatie*, the unleavened native bread, delicious smothered in butter and Oxford marmalade.

Our baggage train resembles the progress of a medieval king. We sahibs only carry what we need for the day (although my rucksack's heavier, with my medical case), but the coolies are astonishing. Each bears a wooden packing crate on his (or her) back, or firewood in a conical basket called a *doko*; each load weighs *eighty pounds*, and is borne suspended from a band across the brow. The tendons of their necks stand out like ropes. God knows what it's doing to their cervical vertebrae.

Lunch is Plasmon biscuits with tinned pâté and Kendal Mint Cake; then we march till four, when the coolies pitch camp. Cotterell and McLellan check supplies, while Garrard gets busy with his cameras and Kits with his gun. Yesterday he shot a red panda for sport, but mostly it's ibex and wild goat.

I'm finding it a strain being with people all the time, so I often wander off with the dog. My pony trod on his paw in the last village, and when I jumped down to make sure it wasn't broken, he got the wrong idea and followed me. He's ridiculously shaggy, like a cross between a collie and a sheep, and he'll fetch anything I throw, as long as it isn't a stick. I call him Cedric, because he has a trick of cocking his head that reminds me of my cousin's husband.

We dine at seven, seated on crates in the mess tent. We're saving the tinned meats for the mountain, so either we slaughter one of the sheep we've brought along, or we feast on whatever Kits has bagged. It all tastes of charcoal and our cook's yak-dung cigarettes.

I'm having a job keeping everyone's digestion in order. I insist on our *chuppaties* being made with English flour, as the native stuff is full of grindstone, and I dispense liver tablets for iron and stewed wild rhubarb for Vitamin C. Yesterday, constipation struck; I was doling out Livingstone Rousers as if they were toffees.

It's too cold at night to undress, and we've reduced washing to what Garrard prettily calls "a French whore's bath": strictly armpits and groin. We're in our tents by eight, and sleep like the dead.

Well, the others do. I'm still having half-awake arguments with Clare. That's pure guilt. The poor girl didn't love me, but she didn't deserve to be jilted.

The bad dreams aren't letting up either, although the snow globe has given way to Charles Tennant in a devil mask. He steals into my thoughts by day, too. I can't forget the terror in his eyes.

These wretched nightmares. I don't *think* I've woken any of the others, although once or twice I've heard someone in another tent cry out in his sleep. I think it's Cotterell. Perhaps he was more affected by the trenches than I thought.

Or perhaps, like me, it's this country. This unreality.

I still have no idea why it happened.

Yesterday, we camped at thirteen thousand feet on a desolate moor called Dzongri, where McLellan paid off most of the lowland coolies, and took on the yak-wallahs.

I was glad to leave Dzongri. It's supposed to be particularly spirit-haunted, and I didn't care for the *chortens* that seemed to watch us from the hills.

But I took to the yaks at once. They're like small, immensely shaggy bulls with extravagant horns and flowing, horse-like tails. You always know where they are because of the dull clank of their bells; and they're as placid as oxen. Except when they're not.

We were on a trail halfway up a steep-sided gorge when one of them panicked. I saw it happen. The beast spotted something above it on the slope and simply went wild, bucking and rolling its white-rimmed eyes. Before the coolies could do anything, it had blundered off the trail and crashed all the way to the bottom, where it lay, twitching and grunting, until a yak-wallah skittered down and cut its throat with his *kukri*.

The crates it was carrying were smashed to splinters. "Christ bugger *fuck!*" exploded Garrard. "That's the wireless *and* the cinematographic camera! *Fuck!*"

"That's enough," snapped Cotterell, who has a spinsterish dislike of bad language. "We mightn't have got reception at the mountain anyway, it could've been worse."

Not for the yak-wallah, it couldn't. Yak-wallahs are so poor they don't even own a bedroll; they sleep wrapped in their beast's saddle-cloth. I slipped the man twenty rupees — that's about three weeks' pay — and he bowed as he cradled it in both hands. His deference made me feel ashamed.

The yak was butchered where it lay, and soon all that remained were bones, some bluish entrails that even coolies won't eat, and a great splash of scarlet on the rocks.

Ravens appeared from nowhere, cawing like birds of ill omen. I had to restrain Cedric from chasing them.

Nima told me their Nepalese name is *gorak*. "There will be more as we go higher, Doctor Sahib." I couldn't tell if he thought that was good or bad.

I wonder what spooked that yak. There was nothing on that slope. I know because I happened to be looking right at it when the beast panicked. So what frightened it?

And how *quickly* it happened. The yak was alive, then it was dead. It's a warning: this land is dangerous.

But it's a *physical* danger. I'm not afraid of that.

I can't get used to how cramped it is in my tent.

I dislike the way my torch stabs the darkness as I squirm into my sleeping bag, and the shut-in sounds of rustling and breath. I hate being so enclosed when I tighten the drawstring around my face. I always end up poking my head out and pulling on my balaclava instead.

Tonight, my tent stinks. My kitbag was part of the dead yak's load, and despite Nima's best efforts, it reeks of blood; although at least it didn't seep through.

Perhaps that's why I sleep even worse than usual. Muffled voices and half-heard footsteps bleed into my dreams, and I keep fancying that someone's there: someone outside the tent, standing in silence, unnervingly close. It's because I'm half asleep, of course, but it's peculiarly alarming. That's what I dislike most about tents: you can't see what's coming.

I'm just drifting off when I'm jolted awake by thudding hooves and the clang of yak bells.

Drowsily, I listen to muffled cries and the patter of bare-foot coolies. Sounds as if one of the beasts is running amok through camp. Well, I'm too sleepy to stir. Besides, I'm safe in my tent.

No I'm not. If that yak trips on a guy rope, I'll be crushed.

I struggle out of my sleeping bag, but the beast has blundered off. In the adjacent tent, Garrard mumbles in his sleep. Then all is quiet.

When next I drift up to consciousness, it's still dark, and something's moving near my head. The tent is bulging inwards, cold, musty canvas pressing on my face. Moaning, I fight it off with both fists. Then I'm awake — and it's only the dog. He couldn't get inside, so he's burrowed under my groundsheet.

"Bugger off, Cedric," I mumble as my heartbeats return to normal. Outside the tent, the dog heaves himself up and slumps down again, by my feet.

I lie smelling the bitter tang of burning rhododendron, listening to the crackle of the fire and the murmur of coolies. I don't have to get up for another hour, but I will. I've had enough of tents.

All this starting at shadows, it must be the altitude. We're at over fourteen thousand feet. Soon we'll climb to the Kang La, the high pass over the Singalila Ridge; then it's down into Nepal, and on to the glacier.

I'll sleep better down there.

Milky swirls of ice on the track, and a light snow falling as we trudge the final stretch towards the Kang La. The pass is at over sixteen thousand feet, that's nearly the height of Mont Blanc. I'm holding up fairly well, only a little breathlessness. Cedric, plodding beside me, seems fine too; but I'm worried about the coolies, most of whom are still barefoot.

My fellow sahibs aren't doing amazingly, either. Cotterell's panting hard, Garrard's complaining of a headache, and Kits is forging ahead to conceal his breathlessness.

Catching up with him, I ask if he's all right. "Never better," he gasps. But his breath smells, and I suspect he's been sick behind a rock.

I don't want to goad him into further exertion, so I drop behind. "Time to call a halt and issue those boots," I tell McLellan.

"Not till Nepal," he pants.

I stare at him in disbelief. So much for his Christian principles. "Come now, man! It's snowing, these people need — "

"For Christ's *sake*, leave it to me!" He's replaced his topi with a sheepskin flying helmet, which makes him look like an infuriated Biggles; and a blood vessel has burst in his eye, turning it a bright oxygenated scarlet.

"Have you a headache?" I say sharply. "Nausea?"

"Just because I disagree with you doesn't mean I'm ill!"

I turn on my heel and stomp off to find Cotterell. "Call a halt, please, Major, the coolies need boots."

"Not far to the pass," he gasps. "Can't it — "

"No, I'm afraid it bloody well can't!"

McLellan staggers up, his freckled face puce with fury. "How *dare* you go behind my back!"

"That'll do," says Cotterell. Without further discussion, he calls a halt beneath a large rocky overhang, and tells the Scotsman to issue the boots.

The coolies are pathetically grateful, and with the enforced rest, McLellan's temper swiftly improves; he has the grace to look sheepish. That's good, because I need him to translate for me. "And the sahibs need to hear this too," I say tartly.

Once everyone's under the overhang, with a shaggy wall of yaks shielding us from the worst of the elements, I have their attention.

"Mountain sickness," I shout, pausing to let McLellan translate, "attacks *at random*. Old, young, fit — it makes no difference. You're breathless. Your head hurts. You vomit. Can't sleep. Bad dreams. You get

50

angry." I catch McLellan's eye and he reddens. "I can make you feel better — but if it keeps getting worse, the *only* cure is to descend several hundred feet. If you climb higher — you die." I let that sink in. "So if you feel ill, *tell me*! It doesn't make you less of a man . . . or woman," I falter, catching a wry glance from a pretty Sherpani. "Is that understood?"

A general murmuring and shuffling of feet.

"Good. End of lecture."

Well that's cleared the air. I feel better too. All that rot about "unseen spirits" and "birds of ill omen". And being scared of my own *tent*! I've been letting this country affect my nerves. It won't happen again.

I gave Garrard and McLellan phenacetin for their heads, Kits a bromide for his nausea, and we soldiered on — and at long bloody last, we were over the Kang La. The view up there is supposed to be "stupendous" (of course), but all we saw was whirling snow.

What a relief, though, to be going downhill. After a couple of thousand feet, it grew warmer and the snow turned patchy, with drifts of tiny blue gentians. Cotterell has just called a halt at a stretch of levelish ground surrounded by stunted birch trees.

I'm so tired it's taken me a while to notice that the wind is getting up and the coolies are scrambling to pitch camp. The sky has turned an ominous, glassy green, and charcoal clouds are piling in from the north. As if to remind us of its presence, Kangchenjunga is sending us a storm.

There's no time for dinner, I can already hear the boom of thunder stalking us along the ridges. We sahibs grab mugs of tea and chunks of fruit cake, and dive into our tents.

Suddenly the wind's screaming, snow hammering my tent, which is flapping like a live thing. No, not snow, *hail*. Through the little celluloid window in the front flap, I glimpse a birch tree thrashing like a twig in a blue flare of lightning. I'm huddled in my sleeping bag, cradling my mug, with Cedric trying to burrow under my legs, and the lightning flashing, thunder shaking the ground beneath me, but I'm not frightened, I'm *exhilarated*. There's no *point* being scared, there's nothing I can do. If I'm struck, I'll be dead in a heartbeat.

"I say, Stephen!" yells Kits from the adjacent tent. "You might want to put down that mug!"

Oh God, it's tin; he must have seen me silhouetted in the glare. He's hooting with laughter, and so am I as I fling the mug aside. The next instant, I realise how illogical that is, chucking a tin mug when I'm inside a tent with a metal frame, and I laugh even harder. The coolies, crammed in their tents, are laughing too; they're enjoying the storm as much as we. And I love the fact that bloody Lyell never had a storm on *his* trek, not with that "glorious" weather — so this belongs entirely to us.

The storm rages on, and I must have slept, because Nima is waking me with tea and hot buttered *chuppaties*.

52

It's still dark. The tapes of my tent flaps are frozen, but although I don't remember doing it, I tied them with thief knots last night, which means that one good tug does the trick.

Dragging on my stiff, cold boots, I crawl outside amid clouds of frosty breath.

Camp has been transformed by a glittering blanket of snow. The sky is clear and ablaze with stars, so astonishingly bright that I don't need my torch.

The sky is clear. At last I make out the dark bulk of mountains all around. I wish I knew which one is Kangchenjunga.

The storm has settled my nerves as nothing else could. I feel better than I have in months. And for the first time since leaving England, I haven't dreamt at all.

CHAPTER
SIX

The coolies have been making trouble ever since the Kang La.

I've asked Nima what's wrong, and he always gives a different answer. They don't like following Lyell, or they're running out of *tsampa* — "And we can't eat your food, Doctor Sahib" — or simply, "This way is not good." But *why*? I can't shake the feeling that there's something he's not telling me.

Tomorrow, the yak-wallahs return to their village, and five of our Sherpas want to go with them. Cotterell and McLellan are doing their damnedest to dissuade them. I'm keeping out of it. I'd only complicate things, or end up quarrelling with McLellan.

We're camped just west of the glacier, and although we can't see it because of the high ridge of moraine along its flank, it's sending a freezing wind that's making the tents flap; the noise kept us awake last night. Fifty yards off, at the foot of the moraine, a large cairn marks the way to the ice. Tomorrow, we climb past it and head up the glacier. As the *gorak* flies, it's only a few miles to the south-west face of Kangchenjunga.

We can't see that either, because of the guardian peaks. This morning we woke to the first clear skies since Darjeeling — and there they were, right on top of us: the towering sentinels that watch the approach to the mountain.

Cotterell had tears in his eyes; dreaming of the Himalayas had kept him going in the trenches. McLellan doffed his topi and stood staring, his lips soundlessly moving; no doubt if he'd been alone, he'd have knelt in prayer. As for Garrard, Kits and me, we stumbled about like drunks, Garrard laughing, Kits shouting the names of the peaks: "Jannu! Bokroh! Look, Beak, there's Kabru and Rathong — and good Lord, Koktang!"

"My God! My *God!*" I whispered. Wherever I turned, I was assaulted by dizzying heights of fluted ice, a glaring white against an indigo sky. Such immensity. It was overwhelming. I couldn't take it in. Daunting to think that every one of them is thousands of feet *lower* than our mountain.

Until today, these peaks had kept themselves well hidden. After the storm on the Kang La, we had days of rain and fog. We descended through pine forests wreathed in cloud, to the Yalung River. It glided silent and opaque, but the chaos of dead trees along its banks gave a grim foretaste of the torrent it will become in the Monsoon. That's only a few weeks away.

The bridge was down, so young Pasang struggled across with a rope, then we waded through the freezing water, clinging on for dear life. The yaks ploughed stolidly across, and Nima carried Cedric in a *doko,* while Cotterell, who's prone to rheumatism, crossed on the back of his servant: a six-foot Englishman atop a small, staggering Sherpa.

Yesterday, we passed a ruined monastery: the last trace of humanity on our route. It's been abandoned for decades, but it felt as if the monks had only just left. Mossy carvings seemed to exhale long-dead prayers to the mountain: *Please do not blight our crops, please do not drown our village* . . . That's what's frightening the coolies: we're getting close to the mountain.

The others are still arguing with them, so I wander off towards the moraine. I can't resist the pull of that glacier, I *have* to climb up and take a look.

The snow is patchy as I head for the cairn, with clumps of grass poking through. It's the last grass we'll see for weeks. Cedric pads at my heels, occasionally launching a doomed attack on a *gorak*. The ravens allow him within snapping distance, then lift into the air with scornful caws.

I don't know what I'm going to do about Cedric. I feel responsible for him. After all, my pony trod on his paw. But a glacier's no place for a dog.

For the first time in days, I'm *hot*. I can feel the sun beating down on my shoulders through my flannel shirt, and on my head, despite my canvas fishing hat. I've made everyone slather their faces with Penaten glacier cream, but I've stupidly left my snow glasses in my tent, and the glare is eye-watering. What's more, I haven't even reached the cairn and I'm panting. Is it the altitude? After all, we've been climbing since the river, we're at over fifteen thousand feet.

The summit of Kangchenjunga is over *twenty-eight thousand*. That gives me a deep, visceral thrill: half excitement, half dread.

The wind has dropped to nothing, and I catch voices from camp. "No, we have snow gear for everyone." "But I *told* you, we have more than enough *tsampa!*"

I turn my back on them, and once again, I'm alone with the peaks. There's a wildness, a savagery about them that I've never felt in the Alps. They are so astonishingly remote.

I suppose it's because I come from the modern world of telegraphs, aeroplanes and several posts a day, but it's hard to grasp that if I wanted to send a message, it would have to go by mail-runner, and I couldn't hope for a reply within a month.

And yet, though this place strikes me as unearthly, it's not, it's profoundly *earthly*. What's unsettling is that it holds no trace of humanity. In the Alps, there have been times when I've felt isolated, but I've always known that people are only a few hours away. Out here, we might as well be on the moon.

Yesterday, I tried to get this across to the others. "From now on, it's just us and the mountain."

Kits rolled his eyes, and Garrard grinned. "Well, if you don't count ravens, vultures and the odd wild sheep."

"Yes, but you know what I mean, nothing human."

The moraine is a dusty ridge of grey rubble a hundred feet high, haunted by snow pigeons. As I reach the bottom, they lift into the sky, swerving in unison before settling higher up.

The cairn is larger than it appeared from camp; it must be ten feet tall. At its base, the coolies have left the inevitable offerings of incense and little dishes of *ghee*; and long ago, someone jabbed a bamboo pole in its flank, with a line of tattered prayer flags hanging limp.

Cairns always remind me of a friend of Aunt Ruth's, a doughty lady mountaineer of the 1890s who once unfurled a Votes for Women banner on the summit of one of the lesser Himalayan peaks, then placed her card in a jam jar and had her coolies build a cairn over it. How splendidly Victorian, to leave one's visiting card on a mountain!

There's not a breath of wind, and the prayer flags hang lifeless.

The other thing about cairns is that I always feel an ignoble urge to dismantle them and see what's underneath. Idly, I pluck a stone from the base. It's rough with lichen, which crumbles to black dust under my thumb. I replace it with a slight feeling of transgression.

A *gorak* thuds on to the cairn, making me start.

The bird fixes me with a knowing stare. I shoo it away, scolding Cedric for not doing his duty; but he's not here, he must have returned to camp.

The *gorak* has flown off and so have the snow pigeons, leaving me alone with the cairn. Idly, I walk round to the other side.

I didn't expect this. What a disagreeable surprise. There's a plaque affixed with wire at about eye level. It's made of battered aluminium, and seems once to have been a plate of the sort people use for camping; but someone has hammered in an inscription in rusty nails: *Dr Francis A. Yates, 33, d. xx.v. 1906.*

I step back smartly, wiping my palm on my thigh. Until now, Lyell and his companions — apart from old Tennant — have scarcely been real. I've never given a thought to where they might be buried. And yet here before me, beneath this pile of rocks that I won't touch again, lie the remains of a man. A man who was almost the same age as me when the mountain killed him.

All I can call to mind of the tragedy is the bare bones (as it were). They'd climbed within a few thousand feet of the summit when a blizzard forced them to abandon the attempt. For days they were snowed in at an upper camp, and when the weather cleared and they began the descent, an avalanche struck. Lyell and Tennant braved all sorts of dangers to retrieve the dead and wounded — that's why they're heroes — but the injured men died soon after. Poor Dr Yates must have been one of those.

Did he die here, where we're camped, or somewhere on the glacier? If he died on the glacier, perhaps Lyell wanted to bring the body here, rather than simply lowering it into a crevasse. Perhaps he wanted his comrade to be buried beneath earth and grass, out of sight of the mountain.

But what a dreadful, lonely place for a grave! Since the day they laid him to rest, no expedition has entered this valley. I'm the first living man who's stood here in twenty-nine years.

Although on reflection, does that matter? Surely the purpose of a grave is to benefit the living. Aren't the dead beyond caring where they lie?

Whatever I tell myself, the past feels uncomfortably close. This man was a doctor, like me. He made the same trek from Darjeeling that I've just made, then struggled most of the way up the mountain — only to end here, in this desolate place, beneath a pile of rocks. That could be me under there.

Without warning, I'm overwhelmed by an appalling sense of loneliness. Not solitude, nothing so peaceful. What I feel is the howling agony of abandonment . . .

Swiftly, I whistle for Cedric, but he doesn't come. I wish I hadn't whistled; the echoes do nothing to lessen the feeling — which is perfectly ridiculous, with camp only fifty yards off.

Clouds veil the sun, turning the light an unwholesome grey. I've lost all desire to climb the moraine. The air feels heavy and thick; somehow — oppressive. As I'm lighting a cigarette, I hear one of the others coming up behind me. "Look what I've found," I say between puffs. "There's a plaque — "

There's no one there. Not a soul within fifty yards.

In disbelief, I walk round the other side of the cairn. Still no one.

But there *was* someone, I heard him. He was right behind me, I heard the scrape of boots on grit. And I *knew* he was there, I had that unmistakeable feeling you get when you know you're not alone. I can't understand why there's nobody here.

Again, I wipe my hand down my thigh, leaving a dark smudge on my trousers. I step away from the cairn. I clear my throat and stare down at my cigarette.

"Stephen! Hulloa! Stephen!" And there is Kits, halfway up the moraine.

It can't have been him, he's too far away.

"Wake up, Bodge! What are you staring at?"

At last I find my voice. "Come down," I croak. "Take a look at this!"

He skitters down to me in a rattle of pebbles and a haze of grey dust — and of course he's *thrilled* by the plaque, as I knew he would be: it's his first tangible link with one of his heroes.

"*Yates*," he says reverently. "I knew he was buried somewhere around here, but I never *imagined* . . ." Excitedly, he yells for Garrard to come and take photographs, then searches happily for the smallest pebble to pocket as a keepsake.

For once, I'm glad of his noisy enthusiasm. And I'm heartily ashamed of myself. These morbid thoughts about Dr Yates, it simply won't *do*. Imagine how merciless Kits would be if he found out.

And yet, on reflection, I suppose it's only to be expected that I'm a tad out of sorts. The *remoteness* of this place . . . It forces one to confront one's own insignificance as never before. And we are so very far from help. As a doctor, I know better than the others how little I could do if one of us fell ill — or simply fell. All this has just been powerfully brought home to me by this unforgiving pile of rocks — this rather too tangible intimation of mortality.

61

It would be odd if I *didn't* feel alarmed.

Before nightfall, I stroll back to the cairn and add three small pebbles to its base: one to replace Kits' keepsake, and two for him and me; because one oughtn't to pass a cairn without adding a stone. And that's *not* superstition, it's merely a long-established custom, observed by mountaineers around the world.

The sun has gone behind the western peaks, and it's already below freezing. The wind is whipping dust in my eyes and the prayer flags are fluttering forlornly.

I've also come back to prove that I can: that there are no footsteps, and never were.

Silence, apart from the hiss of wind and dust. No sense of someone behind me. And no footsteps.

I suppose the uncomfortable truth is that I'm just as good at denial as anyone else. I've been telling myself that the altitude isn't affecting me, but it is. The altitude, the heat and the glare, they're all doing their work.

And the echoes in this valley are so damned odd.

CHAPTER
SEVEN

I know it's a bad idea to read about climbing disasters, but Kits says there's another cairn coming up, and I want to be proof against any more nonsense.

What do I mean by nonsense? Well I don't mean that I *imagined* those echoes, because I didn't. I mean that it's lack of knowledge which lets in the shadows. The fleeting glimpse causes the brain to weave nightmares — whereas if one turns on the light, then the "something glimpsed", or in my case half heard, becomes thoroughly understood, and the brain is set at ease.

Anyway, I've borrowed Cotterell's pocket history of Himalayan mountaineering. It only has a few pages on Kangchenjunga, and that's all I want: no details, just the facts.

And my God, they're bad enough. All mountains are killers, but ours is worse than most. In the thirty years that white men have tried to conquer it, it's slaughtered twenty-one.

A Swiss-led party made the first attempt in 1905 and lost four, although regrettably not the despicable Crowley, who refused to leave his tent to rescue his dying Sherpas. In '29, an American tried it *alone* and was never seen again; so I wasn't the first at Yates' cairn; that Yankee must have been here six years ago. Then in '30 came the vast Dyhrenfurth/ Smythe show; they attacked the north face, and lost three. And in '31, Bauer's lot also tried the north face, and lost four.

Lyell, back in '06, has the dubious honour of the highest death toll, with nine. Maybe that explains his hold on the popular imagination: that, and the fact that he climbed within a few thousand feet of the summit, which gives his tale a crueller twist. Certainly, as I huddle in my sleeping bag with an electric hand lamp positioned beside Cotterell's little book, I'm just as ghoulishly drawn to their fate as anyone else.

They had climbed to a little over twenty-two thousand feet when, as often happens at altitude, a trivial error triggered disaster. They had paused for a breather when one of them accidentally knocked his rucksack a yard or so out of reach. He then compounded his error by trying to retrieve it alone, slipped and fell to his death. This catastrophe seems to have turned their luck, for soon afterwards, a blizzard forced them to abandon the ascent, and they had to retreat to the camp below, where they were snowed in for three days.

Three days at twenty-two thousand feet! And this was in 1906, before oxygen canisters. All they had for treating mountain sickness was cognac and kola biscuits.

At last the weather cleared, but as they began their descent, an avalanche struck. Edmund Lyell and Charles

Tennant were unhurt; the others were engulfed. What earned Lyell a place of honour in the annals of mountaineering was his dogged refusal to abandon his fallen comrades. He and Tennant braved frostbite, icefalls and a coolie mutiny, and eventually recovered two dead and two alive, albeit terribly injured. After laying the dead to rest at the foot of the mountain, they set off with the injured men. Tragically, during the trek down the Yalung Glacier, both the wounded succumbed.

Shutting the book, I light another cigarette and take a nip of brandy from my flask. So there we are. Precisely the kind of heroic failure at which we British excel. Although for all my cynicism, I do understand why Garrard and Kits revere Lyell. By any standards, it was an astonishing feat.

I find it disturbingly easy to imagine what it was like. The joy on finding two of one's comrades alive in the snow; then the slowly ebbing hope, and finally the heartbreak as first Stratton, then Yates died on the trek.

Enough of this. It's doing me no good at all.

Kits says the Stratton cairn isn't far ahead.

Well I never expected this. The glacier's *horrible*. So much for sparkling pinnacles of ice; it's nothing but rubble. The whole bloody Yalung Glacier is covered in filthy grey rubble, like some gigantic rubbish heap.

Apparently, this is typical of Himalayan glaciers — "Which you'd have known," as Kits helpfully pointed out, "if you'd bothered to do any reading." Well I didn't, and thanks for not warning me in advance.

Two days in, and we've only done five miles. Like some loathsome dragon, the glacier flings obstacles in our way: ridges, crevasses, boulders bigger than cathedrals. It won't even allow us a glimpse of the mountain.

I stay where I'm most needed, with the baggage train, and Cedric plodding along at my heels. I didn't have the heart to send him off with the yak-wallahs, and he seems quite at ease on the glacier, and instinctively knows to avoid crevasses.

My fellow sahibs form the advance party, and trudge ahead with four Sherpas, hammering in pitons, setting ropes up the tricky parts, and marking the route with cairns. *More* bloody cairns. I do wish they'd use flags.

So far, we've crossed dozens of crevasses; thank Heavens McLellan thought to bring ladders. They sag alarmingly as we walk or crawl across, trying to ignore the echoing gurgles far below. We're roped, of course, but it's a point of honour not to wobble, and that's hard, with one's ice-axe swinging by its safety loop, and Nima behind, carrying Cedric in a *doko* and muttering prayers against the *mirgút* — a sort of "Abominable Snowman" who lurks in the depths and drags men to their doom.

I've decided that the best way of dealing with Nima's superstitions is to tolerate them. Besides, there's a lot more to him than that. I think he and Pasang are related — although you'd never guess to look at them, young Pasang being quite extraordinarily handsome, with aquiline features and finely cut nostrils that would be the pride of an archduke. But the assistant *sirdar* treats the older man with deference, as do the other Sherpas, and I'm beginning to see why. Yesterday, I was behind Nima when we were traversing a particularly difficult stretch, and as soon as I started putting my feet where he did, it became much easier and less laborious.

I shall be overjoyed to see the back of this glacier. At night, the temperature plunges to twenty below, but by day it's an oven. One goes from frostbite to sunstroke in half an hour.

I'm turning into a bit of a fusspot. Well, I have to be, it's my job. I remind everyone to drink, even if they're not thirsty, and to prevent chills, I make them carry a spare shirt in their rucksacks, and change the moment we stop. I also insist on hats, snow glasses and glacier cream, especially for McLellan with his freckles, and Garrard with his thinning fair hair and beaky nose (it's peeling, of course). With our white faces and blank black eyes, we sahibs resemble those ghouls from the devil dance — albeit with beards.

By far the worst thing, though, is that there's no wind, and the air feels heavy, and strangely *dead*. I've read about "glacier lassitude", it's a Himalayan peculiarity, but I never thought it would be so unpleasant. I've a thumping headache and I'm tired all the time.

Every afternoon, we pitch camp with the guardian peaks frowning down on us, and below them, the great, silent, uninhabited valleys. Now and then, there's a distant boom, and an avalanche claws its way down from the heights. That's why we're keeping to the middle.

Our nights are noisy. If it isn't an avalanche, it's the ice around us creaking and groaning, as if something's struggling to get out. I'd find it disturbing if I didn't feel so rotten.

I hate feeling like this when the others don't, and I'm doing exactly what I told them not to: I'm pretending I'm fine. I dole out aspirin for the coolies' headaches, ammonium chloride for Garrard and McLellan's mild lassitude, and a bromide for Cotterell, who's a tad worse. Of course, bloody fucking Kits is "absolutely top-hole". (Ill temper is another symptom, and I really ought to stop swearing, but it helps, so I don't think I shall.)

The one *good* thing is that I've just passed the Stratton cairn without even noticing. I only realised what it was when I glanced back and saw Garrard and Kits taking photographs. For form's sake, I sent Nima to give the thing a stone on my behalf. And I was glad to see that Cedric padded past without turning his head; so clearly, he sensed nothing untoward.

Well of course he didn't, it's a pile of rocks. I blame our old nurse for the fact that such nonsense ever crossed my mind. She used to say that people built cairns to stop the dead from walking. What *rot*. It annoys me that I should have remembered that now.

I can't believe how much better I feel. The headache's gone. And it snowed in the night; the glacier is *transformed*. All day we've been picking our way around my longed-for pinnacles. Some are a surreally dazzling white, while others have a strange, blue, wind-polished glisten. And there are lakes, too, of the purest, bluest blue you ever saw.

The snow is knee-deep, but the advance party trudges ahead, breaking trail, so we in the baggage train are having it easy. "One could take a pram up this," remarks McLellan, "and not even bruise the baby's bottom."

This afternoon, we camped on the eastern edge of the glacier, behind a big spur of moraine which will, we hope, protect us from avalanches. Kabru is behind us now, and to the right rises Talung, the final peak before our mountain. Kangchenjunga is only a couple of miles away — although still out of sight.

It's a glorious afternoon, and I've just spent a marvellous two hours alone in my tent, varnishing my sphygmograph readings. After weeks of enforced *camaraderie*, a little solitude has left me feeling calm and happy, like a glass that's been refilled with clear water.

The others are still having tea in the mess tent (with Cedric begging shamelessly for scraps), and I'm heading off to climb that spur, and see what I can see. I mean the mountain, of course, but I daren't name it, not even to myself. I don't want to jinx my chances of seeing it at last.

We're at seventeen thousand feet, but I'm fighting fit, no more ghastly glacier lassitude. My breath is loud and strong as I crunch up the pebbly moraine. In the distance, there's a sound like an express train. I think that's the wind roaring over the peaks. The sun is scorching, but a chill westerly breeze is keeping me cool: no dead air here!

About twenty feet above me, a flock of choughs is squabbling over something in the rocks. After scaring them off, I come upon a scattering of bleached bones. It looks like one of those wild blue sheep — which in fact aren't blue at all, but a disappointing grey. I'm out of breath, so I throw myself down by the bones. And suddenly there it is. Kangchenjunga.

Photographs fail utterly to convey its power. From my perch on the spur, the glacier leads towards it like a shimmering royal road — although that's putting a human gloss on something which has nothing to do with humanity. Up and up my eye climbs, past sweeping, dark-red precipices and glaring white ice, to those immaculate peaks, the highest trailing a banner of wind-blown snow across a sky so intensely blue that it's almost black.

Kangchenjunga.

It takes me with a twist of the heart that makes me gasp. *How* could I not have realised? The moment I saw it, my adult self peeled away and I was a boy again, gazing in awe at the Crystal Mountain in the fairy tale. It's never gone away, it's always been there, deep inside me, this longing for the summit. *Like seen music*, some climber once said.

This is why I came. Not to escape the mess back home, but for *this*. It was always and only ever about this.

Someone touches my shoulder, and with a cry I lurch round.

It's Garrard and Kits. I can see from Garrard's ugly, transfigured features that it's the same for him. "M-my God," he falters. "Lyell was right . . . All other mountains are female — but Kangchenjunga is simply 'It'."

Kits mops his brow with his handkerchief and gives an embarrassed laugh. "Big, isn't it?"

Garrard, the dutiful friend, forces a smile. I don't. I can't. My throat has closed. No words come.

Kits shoots me an impatient glance. He loathes displays of emotion; he thinks they're bad form.

As we watch, there's a distant boom, and ice breaks from the Face of the mountain, shattering to powder on the lower cliffs and sending great white snow clouds billowing upwards. Kangchenjunga is giving us a show of force.

Garrard and I exchange apprehensive glances, but Kits, ever the climber, is already studying the Face through his field glasses.

I ask for a turn, but he doesn't respond. I suppress a twinge of irritation at being demoted to the importunate younger brother: *Oh please, Kits, let me have a go!*

When at last he hands me the glasses, it's a shock to see the mountain up close. What to the naked eye appeared so beautiful is in fact horrific beyond belief. The tallest peak is blurred by snowstorms; I can almost hear the screaming wind. Below it, there's a dreadful plunge to a gigantic ice shelf that slashes horizontally across the Face. Beneath that, appalling red granite precipices drop sheer for thousands of feet. To the left of these, ice tumbles from the end of the shelf like a vast frozen waterfall, down past a massive triangular buttress of stark black rock, and on to the glacier below.

But the mountain's very cruelty only makes me want it more. I don't give a damn what Kits says, it's unthinkable that I won't be part of the team for the summit. This is why I came.

Only this.

CHAPTER
EIGHT

Base Camp at last!

We've only been here a few hours, but already it feels like home. We've built a windbreak of packing crates around the sahibs' and mess tents, with the coolies' quarters downwind, near the cook-site and stores dump. From now on, this is GCHQ: an island of safety in all this immensity.

Cotterell and McLellan wanted to pitch Base on the rocky knoll just left of the Buttress, as that's where we'll be starting the climb. Kits wanted it too, as it's where Lyell had *his* Base, but the coolies flatly refused, because it's also the site of the remaining Lyell graves. Thank Heavens for that. Who wants the shark's fin of the past jutting into the present?

So instead, we're camped half a mile in *front* of the Buttress, which means we're still on the glacier, but protected from rolling avalanche débris by several giant boulders. Behind us and on either side are the guardian peaks. Before us, the overwhelming Face. To its right, a saddle-shaped ridge sweeps down, then up to the lesser peak of Talung. It's somewhere on that saddle that the lonely Yankee met his end.

This is a cold camp, and full of noises: the rumble of an avalanche, the relentless crack of canvas, the distant roar of the wind across the Face.

Directly before us towers the massive black wedge of the Buttress, with the Icefall rising like a chaotic staircase to the Great Shelf, impossibly far above. The summit is almost out of sight. The Sherpas call it *Takste*, Tiger Peak, as it's the first to be touched with fire at sunrise.

We're so close to the Face that I can't see it through my tent flap's celluloid window. Instead, I've a view of a small, still lake a short way from camp. I don't care for that lake, it's too quiet. But there we are.

We're at eighteen thousand feet, so I've insisted on three days' rest, to "acclimatise". I think everyone's secretly relieved; even McLellan, who for once seems content to relax his timetable.

We've just had an excellent lunch of pressed tongue, macaroni and cheese with spinach, tinned pineapple, Golden Syrup and Garibaldi biscuits, and we're lounging in the sun outside the mess tent. It's odd to think that back in Darjeeling, I felt like the new boy at school. I'm more at home with them now, even though I've yet to prove myself on the climb.

It helps that we're all such a scruffy lot, in our canvas hats, motoring helmets, cricket sweaters, fishermen's jerseys, Varsity mufflers, breeches, trousers, gaiters and puttees. What Garrard calls our "shrubbery" is decidedly unkempt. His beard is wispy and fair, Kits' is thick and brown, while Cotterell's is a startling silver. (It makes him look older, which I don't think he likes.)

74

Despite lashings of Penaten cream, we're all burnt the colour of mahogany — except for McLellan, whose peeling pink skin creates a bizarre effect with his carroty whiskers.

He's writing a letter to his fiancée, a missionary, and Cotterell is smoking his pipe. Garrard is clacking out a despatch to *The Times* on his typewriter, and Kits is struggling with his portable gramophone — so far without success, thank goodness. I'm grooming Cedric. He was startled at first — he's probably never been groomed in his life — but he's loving it now, slitting his eyes and sleeking back his ears.

Suddenly, there's a deafening boom. I glance up in time to see a gigantic slab of ice breaking off from the Shelf and rushing down the precipice. I see it strike the lower cliffs and shatter to powder. Then I don't see anything because I'm diving with the others into the mess tent.

Seconds later, the shock wave hits, roaring through camp and pummelling the tent.

There's no time to be scared; it's over in moments. We stare at each other as we listen to the rumbles die away.

Camp is several inches deep in snow, but those giant boulders have done their stuff and protected us from débris. The coolies, remarkably unfazed, are already dusting things off. "*Tchum,*" Lobsang the *sirdar* says unnecessarily. Avalanche.

No one's hurt, even Cedric simply shakes himself, and we've lost no gear, except for Kits' gramophone. But for a while, none of us speaks. We're all thinking of those graves on the knoll, and of what an avalanche can do to a man. The mountain has sent us a warning: *That's what I did to the last lot.*

"Poor devils," Garrard says quietly.

Cotterell glances at our taut faces, then clears his throat. "Cribbage," he says briskly.

"And medicinal brandy," I add.

Keep calm, that's the ticket. It doesn't do to dwell on the past. Of course I feel sorry about what happened to Lyell, we all do. But that was then and this is now.

My headache's back with a vengeance. Red-hot needles drilling into my skull, and the slightest noise an agony: Nima playing his wretched flute, Kits whistling as he scrambles up and down those fifty-foot boulders at the edge of camp. He says he's doing it "to keep his hand in," but really he's showing off.

I've got diarrhoea, too. I've been postponing a visit to the latrine pit, but I can't any longer.

As I stagger past the boulder where Kits is "practising", pebbles trickle down and he bellows a warning: "*Below!*"

"*Christ*, Kits, why'd you have to shout?"

"Sorry, old man!" He peers down at me and pulls a face. "You look grim. D'you want a hand?"

"No I bloody don't, I can take a shit on my own!"

A shocked silence. "Sorry."

"Me too," I mutter. "Really. I'm not feeling too grand, that's all."

"You look dreadful."

"And you don't, you lucky bastard, so leave me alone."

I'm so beastly weak that I only just manage to pull down my breeches in time. Cedric trots over, swinging his tail, but I shoo him away, and he slinks off with a wounded look.

Somehow, I make it back and crawl into my sleeping bag. Never felt so rotten in my life. Why doesn't Nima come and *do* something?

The tent flaps stir, but it isn't Nima, it's McLellan. He appears fine, apart from slightly inflamed eyes, so why is he bothering me?

"What d'you need?" I mumble.

"Nothing. I heard you call. Thought you might care for some tea." He places the tin mug within reach.

Touched, I feebly bleat my thanks.

He scratches his orange beard, and asks diffidently if I've taken anything for the pain. It hurts too much to shake my head, so I merely frown.

"Oughtn't you to? Physician heal thyself, sort of thing?" A pause. "I daresay you've heard that a few times before."

I manage a wan smile. "Just a few. Over the years."

"Ah. Well. I'll leave you in peace."

When he's gone, I sip the marvellous strong tea, spilling most of it over myself. I really am pathetic. But I don't know how I'm going to get through the night. I miss Cedric. I've grown accustomed to that mound under the groundsheet, and he hasn't come back since I shooed him away. Worst of all, I'm terrified that I won't get better, that I'll be stuck down here at Base, and never set foot on the mountain.

I don't seem to be in my tent any more, I'm lying out on the ice, surrounded by shaggy white yaks. They're jostling and nosing each other with big damp muzzles, I'm worried that I'll be trampled — but when I try to push them away, they ignore me.

Now they're gone, and I'm inside the snow globe. I'm kneeling and pounding my fists against impenetrable glass, while Clare's disembodied voice coos, "Isn't it *darling?*"

I'm back in my tent, too shaken to open my eyes.

The pain doesn't seem *quite* so appalling. If I lie perfectly still, maybe I'll drift off . . .

"*Below!*"

That shout is agony: bands of hot wire tightening around my skull. *Christ*, why must he *shout*?

Whoever it was, he doesn't do it again. I lie staring into the darkness, listening to the silence.

Something odd about it. It's too dense, too absolute. In the gloom, I make out the wind sucking the sides of my tent in and out — but I can't hear it. Am I still dreaming?

I can't be; I'm fully aware of being curled on my side, with a lump of ice digging uncomfortably into my hip, and the bunched-up sweater I'm using as a pillow scratchy against my cheek.

I'm cold, too, despite my Jaeger combinations and double eiderdown sleeping bag. I can feel my scalp shrinking, pulling the hairs erect.

No one would be climbing in the dark, let alone yelling a warning. And yet I still call out: "What happened? Is anyone hurt?"

My voice sounds rough and hesitant. There's no reply. But abruptly, I can hear again. The crack of canvas, the wind whining in the guy ropes.

"Who shouted?" I call.

At last, Nima puts his head in. "Doctor Sahib?"

"Someone shouted."

His woolly yellow cap is askew, and in the glimmer of his candle-lantern, his dark eyes meet mine with respectful curiosity. "Nobody shout, Doctor Sahib. Everybody sleep."

Of course they're asleep, it's two in the morning. It was only one of those dreams which one has on the edge of waking, and which can seem so astonishingly real.

Feeling foolish, I tell Nima he can go. I lie watching his light fade, and the darkness close in. I'm completely alert, my ears straining for the faintest sound.

I wish I hadn't sent him away. I wish Cedric was here. I wish I had light.

I grope for my electric torch, and hold it against my chest. But somehow, I don't like to switch it on.

That cry happened. It wasn't a dream. I heard it.

Poor old McLellan, what rotten luck.

I slept till ten, and woke feeling blessedly better. I ate five *chuppaties* slathered in butter and gooseberry jam, and downed three mugs of tea so strong you could trot a mouse on it, as Cook used to say.

I was tackling the last *chuppatie* when Pasang came running. "Quick, Doctor Sahib, there is fall!"

McLellan was returning from the latrine pit when he tripped. His ankle's fine, but in breaking his fall, he also broke his wrist. So that's his hopes dashed before we've even begun.

It was a nasty fracture, and I gave him a stiff dose of Veramon. He put a brave face on it and even tried to joke: "You chaps had better look out up there, I'll be running the show from Base!" But later, I found him reading his bible with rigid concentration.

When he saw me, he gave a wan smile. "Afraid not even the Good Book's helping right now."

"It's the most rotten luck. Painkiller doing its stuff?"

"Oh yes, grand." But he was lying. I used to be a bit *blasé* about fractures, until I broke my ankle in the Dolomites. I couldn't believe the pain.

"I s'pose it's for the best," McLellan said quietly. "I never did fit in with the rest of you."

"My dear fellow — "

"Well it's true, isn't it?" He forced a laugh. "Minor public school, desk job in military admin. Not quite-quite. As they say."

"You couldn't be more wrong! You're absolutely one of us and we depend on you most frightfully!"

I feared I'd overdone it, but he looked at me with such a hopeful expression. He really wanted to believe. I felt a heel for not liking him more.

Fortunately, our first mail-runner arrived, which cheered us immensely. He appeared as a distant speck on the glacier, and brought a green canvas post bag secured with red sealing wax, packed with news from home. The others had letters from wives and girlfriends, including three from McLellan's missionary fiancée, which bucked him up a bit. I had a nicely acerbic one from Cousin Philippa, and no writ from Clare's father, thank God.

The fly in the ointment was Kits. He took great pains not to mention Dorothy and the boys in front of me, which only drew attention to the fact that I'm the one sahib who's unattached. He did it on purpose, of course, to embarrass me, because he was angry: before lunch, I asked Cotterell to consider me for the summit. Cotterell was delighted, but Kits was furious. He seems to regard the summit as his. He doesn't want his little brother muscling in.

Tea has been and gone, and I'm outside my tent in glorious sunshine, with Cedric at my feet; apparently, I'm forgiven for having shooed him away last night. I'm sorting my latest batch of sphygmograph readings. Considering the altitude, everyone's pulse curves are remarkably normal, even poor old McLellan's — although in view of how grim I felt last night, I've been teaching Nima and Pasang emergency first aid. They're proud of their Red Cross armbands, and Pasang's already better at bandaging than me.

The sun is scorching hot, but there's a chill wind, accompanied by the usual rather maddening bang-bang of canvas, and that express-train roar across the Face, which never stops. Every so often, I hear the distant boom of an avalanche. Mostly they're on Talung or the

Saddle, but several times the Great Shelf has sent one down, and we've braced for the blast.

There's something hypnotic about the Face. Last night, I watched darkness creeping up it like a black tide. And on our first morning here, I saw Tiger Peak glare scarlet. For an instant, the Great Shelf and the precipices seemed tinged with blood. Then veils of snow-fog crept over the summit and down the Face, like something alive.

When I look at the Face, I experience the same dread and desire I felt as a boy, gazing at that picture in the storybook. I can't remember the story itself, but I remember that picture. Three knights riding their chargers up the Crystal Mountain, in search of treasure. One has almost reached the top; his horse's hooves are striking sparks. A second topples backwards to his doom. A third lies dead at the bottom.

Strange that we say the mountain has a "face", when it's really just a pile of rock and ice. It seems that even we Europeans can't resist the urge to personify. Does that make us the same as the Sherpas, with their snow demons? Is all this personifying simply a way of rendering things less frightening? If the mountain has a face, it is amenable to reason, and if we treat it with respect, it won't kill us. The alternative — which I happen to believe is the truth — is that it's all just chance, and we're throwing dice for our lives.

The Sherpas say that the summit is the haunt of a vengeful snow god, *Kang-my*. To appease him, they've painted a prayer on a giant boulder near the lake, and draped it with strings of flags in the four directions of the wind.

Garrard views all this with detached interest and wry amusement. Cotterell, ever the leader of men, tolerates it because it reassures them. Kits dismisses it as childish tosh, as no doubt would McLellan, if he didn't feel so rotten. For myself, I seem to have lost some of my revulsion at their beliefs. Perhaps because I've realised that I can't fight them.

Tomorrow, we're walking to the grave knoll to spy out the route. (I do wish everyone would stop calling it the grave knoll. It's simply a knoll where there happen to be graves, they are not its defining feature.) But oddly enough, the Sherpas seem more worried about the lake. They won't draw water from it for fear of offending the spirits, and when Nima washes my clothes, he insists on trudging half a mile to *another* lake, which for some reason he doesn't regard as haunted.

What must it be like to believe that the entire landscape is watching you? That before moving so much as a rock, you have to propitiate the demon you're about to displace?

They even regard *goraks* as suspect. Just now, one perched on my tent, and Nima chased it away.

I feel sorry for him and his countrymen. It must be dreadful to live in fear of your surroundings.

Although I suppose I'm not exactly immune from fancy, myself. That cry in the night. Shortly after I heard it, McLellan broke his wrist. It feels as if we've been warned.

CHAPTER
NINE

Now that I'm on the grave knoll, I'm even more relieved that we didn't camp here.

Of course, in many ways it would've made an ideal Base. It's rock instead of ice, which makes it warmer, and it's far more convenient, as it's where we'll be starting the climb. But it feels as if Lyell has only just left.

For some reason, there are *two* graves, a smallish oblong cairn with a rough wooden cross, and a larger one with two rusty ice-axes laid rather unsettlingly at the foot. Garrard tells me the smaller is for someone called Pache (he gives it two syllables and a guttural "ch", as in "loch"), while the larger is for Freemantle and Knight. He's about to say more, but I cut him short. "No thanks, I've heard enough."

He grins. "You're really nothing like Kits, are you?"

I shake my head and laugh.

With Cedric at my heels, I wander off, leaving the others taking photographs of the graves. Even Cotterell's joining in. I'm surprised at him, it's the last thing they should be doing on the eve of the climb.

Yates, Stratton, Pache, Freemantle and Knight. I wish I didn't know their names; it makes them so disagreeably *real*. Still, it's a relief to have all five accounted for. No more unpleasant discoveries. From now on, we can concentrate on the mountain.

We left before dawn to reduce the risk of avalanche, and as it's still early, we're in the icy shadow of the Buttress, and exposed to the cutting west wind. The top of the knoll is almost flat, and the size of several cricket pitches. My boots crunch as I pick my way over black, lichen-crusted rocks.

At last I'm actually standing on the mountain itself; albeit right at its feet. It is so immense I can't take it in. I can't see the Great Shelf because the Buttress blocks the view, but from where I stand, a vast wrinkled snow slope sweeps upwards, past the Buttress's west flank, to join the upper reaches of the Icefall, which tumbles down the other side. This snow slope doesn't *appear* that steep, but when I follow it through my field glasses, it keeps rising; it must be three thousand feet high. I feel a spurt of panic: the true panic terror of the wild.

Turning my back on the mountain, I locate Base Camp, half a mile off on the glacier. The sahibs' tents are a neat row of oxblood red, the porters' larger green ones huddled around the cook-site. They look so insignificant. Like chunks of rubble.

I don't care for the knoll. Everywhere I turn, I see traces of Lyell. Over there are the remains of an old shelter wall, and the rectangular patches where they pitched their tents, still littered with rusty paraffin tins and bits of broken packing crate. There's even an old chutney jar, with *Crosse & Blackwell* faintly legible on the label. I can almost see Lyell and his companions: smoking, reading letters from home, eagerly scanning the mountain that would kill them.

Suddenly, I'm gripped by the same appalling sense of loneliness I felt at the Yates cairn. It's as if I've been abandoned by my fellows and left here in this desolate place, with no hope of ever finding my way back.

It's completely irrational. That's what's alarming. Because I'm *not* alone. Here's Cedric, sniffing that chutney jar — and there are the others, poking about near the graves.

Cotterell calls my name. "Come over here and help with the route!"

The feeling is gone as abruptly as it came. By the time I join them, I'm myself again.

Soon the four of us are peering through our field glasses. Once more, I follow the snow slope up to the tip of the Buttress and beyond, to where it becomes a dazzling Cubist chaos of ice. That's the upper part of the Icefall, which leads to the Great Shelf.

All my desire comes roaring back. In a few days, I'll be there. A few days after that, I will stand on the summit.

"Not much doubt about the start," murmurs Cotterell. "We follow Lyell up this snow slope and pitch Camp One where he did. That ledge on the flank of the Buttress, at about — what, Kits, nineteen thousand feet?"

"Nineteen thousand, seven hundred and fifty."

A fond glance from Cotterell. *That's my boy.*

"Next bit looks tricky," says Garrard. "Above the Buttress we'll need to cross the Icefall and head up its eastern edge."

To the naked eye, the upper Icefall appears wrinkled, but through field-glasses, each "wrinkle" is revealed as a towering pinnacle of ice.

"Might be a levelish patch under that crag," I venture.

"Where?" say Garrard and Cotterell together.

"Just right of that big zigzag crevasse — see that crag of darkish ice? A sort of whale-back curve? Under that."

There's a silence, which lasts a while.

"You're thinking of that for Camp Two," says Garrard.

I shrug. "Worth a try."

"No," says Kits.

I look at him. "Why?" He's scarcely said a word to me all morning, and now this. He can't still be sulking because I want a shot at the summit?

"Because it's a bad idea," he replies, still scanning the slope.

"I don't agree," I say evenly. "That crag would provide shelter from avalanches."

He snorts. "You're the medic, Stephen. Why don't you stick to that?"

I'm about to snap back when Cotterell intervenes. "Let's leave it, shall we, gentlemen? The important thing is to establish Camp One. We'll have a better view from there."

"Shouldn't take long," Garrard puts in smoothly. "We can cut steps up most of this snow slope and set ropes for the Sherpas. I'd say a couple of days to get a supply line up and running to Camp One. It'll be easier now that poor old McLellan's managing things from Base."

Cotterell's nodding. "Good show. I want to aim for Advance Base on the Shelf within a week. Once that's well stocked, we'll lay siege to the summit from there."

He makes it sound like army manoeuvres on Salisbury Plain, and Garrard and I exchange wry grins. Kits is still stonily scanning the slope. Well, let him. He'll get over it.

At that moment, the sun kindles the slope above us, and I forget about Kits. What I've seen only makes me want the mountain more. If we take things steadily and the Monsoon doesn't come early, we can do this.

The trouble with Kits is that everything in his whole life has come too easily. Head of House and Captain of the First Eleven at Winchester, star of the Cambridge Mountaineering Club, no need to work because of the Trust — and to cap it all, the beautiful Dorothy, who duly presented him with the regulation brace of boys, and who wouldn't *look* at another man even if a millionaire made a play for her — although actually that's a bad example, as she's a millionaire's daughter.

Yes, for Kits, life has simply unrolled before him like some gorgeous tapestry. So it must come as a nasty shock when one of the lesser threads in that tapestry, namely his brother, doesn't behave precisely as he ought.

Back at Base, I took him aside and asked him why his nose was out of joint. "Ye gods, Kits, we're not in competition! I *know* you're a better climber than me, but why shouldn't I have a shot at the summit as well as you?"

"Because you're not good enough," he said flatly.

"*What?*"

"You're not good enough."

"That's for Cotterell to decide, not you."

"Come off it, Bodge. I wouldn't have asked you along if you weren't a jolly decent climber — but this is *Kangchenjunga!* You're not up to the summit!"

He's always done this. If I ever come close to equalling him, he slaps me down — although always, of course, for the best of reasons.

"You know as well as I do," he went on, pulling his mouth down like a pompous bulldog, "that one must be able to rely on one's fellow climbers a hundred per cent — "

"What the *hell* is that supposed to mean?"

"It means you're not prepared."

"*What?* I trained for weeks on the ship, I'm every bit as fit as you — "

"I don't mean that, I mean you haven't bothered to study Lyell's route. It's not hero-worship that made me read him till I know it backwards, it's common sense! When we were discussing Camp Two back there, you didn't even know that the site you suggested is where Lyell was snowed in! Hardly the luckiest place for us to camp, eh? Garrard and Cotterell knew. They were *embarrassed* for you."

I stared at him. "And you didn't think to tell me at the time."

He snorted. "What do I care if you make a fool of yourself?"

I opened my mouth to reply, then shut it again. For a moment, we regarded each other coldly, like strangers, and the rocks that are always beneath the surface felt very close indeed. One word from me would have sparked a row — and that would have been disastrous. So instead, I turned on my heel and walked away.

I've fetched up here at the lake, seething and pacing up and down. I can hear him at the other end of camp, teaching the Sherpas to belay. He and a young man called Tenrit are roped together, and Kits has seated Tenrit in front of a rock, with the rope looped around it.

"So now," he explains in a singsong voice, as if they're children, "if I climb down below Tenrit, and I slip and he can't hold me, that loop around the rock will hold *him* — which means I won't pull us both off the mountain!"

Dutiful grins for the Great Teacher Sahib, who — Cotterell, please note — remains his usual cheery self, despite unwarranted provocation from his beastly younger brother.

It's noon, and the sun is fierce. The wind has dropped, and on the boulder, the prayer flags hang motionless. The lake is utterly still.

Over the years, we've evolved a way of rubbing along together, and for the most part, it works — *provided* I ignore his half-jocular, half-resentful digs at "medics" and anything remotely "high-brow" that I happen to enjoy, and we restrict our talk to climbing, Aunt Ruth, Dorothy and their two fat, unappealing progeny, as well as every other crashingly boring detail of his crashingly boring life. Only in the odd unguarded moment does the truth ever threaten to erupt: that if we weren't related, we wouldn't give each other the time of day.

But I *knew* all this when I came, so what's changed?

I suppose what I didn't realise is how Kits views my role on the expedition. He thinks we're still at Winchester. He thinks I'm still Pearce *minor*, the clever if slightly awkward younger brother who's only good at things like Latin and Greek, for which no decent fellow cares a fig. He thinks I ought to remain meekly at Base — or at best, the lower camps — while the *real* climbers get on with the job.

The belaying lesson is over, and the Sherpas have returned to the cook-site. Nothing disturbs the peace. No avalanche, no icefall. Not even a *gorak*.

Half of the lake is covered by a thin glaze of greenish-grey ice, which the wind has roughened to an odd, reticulate pattern. The other half is open water, and as still as a looking glass. It mirrors the mountain with photographic clarity. I can see the Great Shelf cutting across the Face, and at its near end, the Icefall tumbling down the right flank of the Buttress, with the snow slope on the other side. On the upper part of the Icefall, I fancy I can just make out that zigzag crevasse, and the dark, whale-backed crag that sparked the row.

The row which, as I squat by the water's edge, now seems embarrassingly childish, a brotherly tiff that we allowed to get out of hand.

The water is extraordinarily clear. I shift focus from the mountain's reflection to what lies beneath: smooth grey pebbles on greenish-gold sand. Cupping water in my palm, I take a sip. It has a mineral tang, and it's so cold it sets my teeth on edge.

Belatedly, I remember Nima's prohibition against drinking from the lake. I can't help smiling. Poor old Nima. He's too polite to scold, but if he knew what I've just done, he'd get his concerned look. Once again, the puppy in his charge has done something unwise.

The sun goes in behind a cloud, and suddenly I'm cold. Something feels wrong. There's a tension in the air. I take a deep breath, but I'm still breathless: a sick, prickling weight on my chest, like the moment before you faint.

I can't hear the Sherpas at the cook-site, or the distant roar of the wind across the Face. The silence feels dense and hostile.

I shift focus from the bottom of the lake to the looking-glass mountain on its surface.

I stop breathing. There's someone up there. Up on the mountain. I can see him, a dark head peering from the crag.

But there can't be anyone that high. There can't be anyone at all.

I lurch round to stare at the mountain itself — and of course he's gone, because he was never there. And yet, some impulse makes me shout, "*Hulloa!* You up there, what d'you want!"

My voice rings out, and at the cook-site, the Sherpas raise their heads and stare.

Turning back to the looking-glass mountain in the lake, I follow the black wedge of the Buttress to its apex, then across the Icefall to the crag.

It's still there. On the mountain. I watch it peering down. Then, slowly, it sinks backwards. Out of sight.

CHAPTER
TEN

It can't have been a bird; it was bigger than that. Or an ibex or a sheep. I asked McLellan if there are any animals on the mountain and he said no, there's nothing alive up there.

Obviously it can't have been a man. And even if it was — *even if*, which isn't possible — I couldn't have seen him, not from that distance; my eyesight's not good enough, no one's is. So it must have been a shadow, or a rock, or an odd formation of ice.

It's three forty-five a.m. and Nima has just brought my tea and *chuppaties*. He didn't need to wake me, I wasn't asleep. I think I did sleep for a few hours, but mostly I lay in that half-conscious muddle which is so much more tiring than being awake.

Yates, Stratton, Pache, Freemantle and Knight. The names tumbled through my mind with a nagging sense that I'd got something wrong. But they're all accounted for, all safe in their cairns. That's what my brain kept assuring me with its warped dream logic. As if a pile of rocks could stop the dead from walking.

It's the tenth of May, the first day of the climb. I really don't wish to know whether that's the same day on which Lyell set off — although doubtless Kits will tell me if it is.

My tent is dark and freezing. The canvas is crusted with hoarfrost. My beard and sleeping bag are stiff with it. From now on, we'll be starting each day well before dawn, to avoid what Cotterell calls the "enemy fire" of rockfall and avalanche.

That's fine with me, the earlier the better. I want as much reality as I can get, even if it does mean waking in darkness and forcing swollen feet into frozen boots. My hands aren't steady, but that's all right too, I always get the shakes before a climb.

Cedric pokes in his nose. I let him in and give him my last *chuppatie*. His eyes are a warm, chocolatey brown, and when I bury my face in his shaggy white scruff, his doggy smell is immensely reassuring.

The others are already outside, stamping in clouds of frosty breath. It's bitterly cold, and the pale yellow shafts of our electric headlamps only deepen the darkness.

Above us, a blizzard of stars in a clear black sky. Without wirelessed reports from Darjeeling, we're relying on Sherpa weather lore, which is proving surprisingly accurate. They say it'll be calm for at least the next few days.

Kits is explaining something interminable about his crampons to Garrard, who, ever the devoted friend, is feigning interest. He looks nervous. The shadows around his close-set eyes are more pronounced, as if he hasn't slept.

Cotterell and McLellan are chivvying the coolies, who are still at that boulder by the lake, casting *tsampa* and singing their tuneless prayers. For once, McLellan doesn't seem to mind. Perhaps he's been praying, too.

All twelve Sherpas will be climbing with us. They're a tight-knit bunch, and most of them seem to be related. Nima is uncle, brother, cousin or some sort of in-law to just about all of them. The other coolies, under McLellan's command, will be running supplies between the lower camps and Base.

And now we're off. It's a two-hour hike to the knoll, and Cedric's coming too, as I knew he would.

"Not sure about that, Dr Pearce," says Cotterell. "He'll be a drain on supplies." He turns to McLellan, who's coming as far as the knoll to see us off. "When you return to Base, old chap, you'll have to take the hound."

"Absolutely, sir." But behind the Major's back, the Scotsman tips me a wink. He's guessed that Cedric will be doing nothing of the sort.

And why *shouldn't* the beast come with us, if he wants to? On the north face, Bauer took a dog to twenty-four thousand feet. Besides, it would give me a chance to compare human and canine physiologies. *And* he's good for morale. Especially mine.

Because the truth is, I *need* Cedric. What I saw yesterday is cutting me off from the others. Oddly enough, McLellan seems to understand that, even though he doesn't know why.

I wish I'd told him last night, when I had the chance.

At dinner I was too shocked and confused to talk to anyone. But later, when I stopped by McLellan's tent to check on him, he asked me if anything was up.

I was startled. "What do you mean?"

He looked embarrassed. "Oh, I don't know. You didn't say much at dinner. You seemed sort of — well, spooked."

" — Spooked," I repeated inanely.

With a rueful smile, he held up his splinted forearm. "This isn't an omen, you know. I mean, for the climb. It was my own stupid fault."

It flashed across my mind that now was my chance to tell him. I could make light of it: *Queerest thing happened to me by the lake. Isn't it odd what one's brain conjures up on the eve of a climb?* And then we could laugh about it, and I could put it behind me.

Instead, I patted his shoulder and forced a smile. "You weren't stupid, old man, just damned unlucky. And don't worry about me, I don't believe in omens."

And that's true, I don't. But I find it alarming that I missed my chance to tell him. After all, what I glimpsed on that crag can't have been anything, so why did I keep quiet?

Well, because — because I don't want anyone thinking the altitude is affecting my nerves. Especially not Kits. He'd pounce on it, and then where would I be? Stuck at Base, that's where.

I just wish it hadn't moved. I can see it now, sinking out of sight. Too slow for a fall, more of a conscious withdrawal. And the *way* it moved . . . It wasn't right.

I keep pushing it out of my mind, but it always comes back. I won't say that I'm scared. Only apprehensive. I can't seem to shake off the feeling that there's something up there, waiting for us.

And I *know* that's impossible; it's simply oxygen lack affecting my perceptions — and doubtless also the Sherpas' odd beliefs, which have been preying on my mind. As well as those infernal Lyell graves.

Just now, as we reached the knoll, Nima lit sticks of incense before each cairn, and whipped off his woolly cap and bowed. On impulse, I went and dropped a pebble on each one; swiftly, and without looking at the names. For luck.

That pleased Kits. I think he took it as a peace offering: my way of honouring Lyell. So once again, things are patched up between us. We've buried the ice-axe, as it were. And that's good, because from now on, it's us against the mountain. Garrard, Kits, Cotterell and me.

I do feel sorry for McLellan. If I was the poor beggar being left at Base, I'd be devastated. And strangely enough, I find that incredibly comforting, because it tells me that I'm *not* so fearfully shaken by what I saw yesterday, and I do still desperately want to climb this mountain.

Even if our route does take us directly over that crag.

Nothing like climbing to drive out the demons.

The weather's *perfect*: sunny, but with enough wind and cloud to prevent the heat becoming unbearable. We're aiming to hack steps up the snow slope and pitch

Camp One where Lyell did, about two thirds up the Buttress' west flank.

Garrard, Kits and I form the advance party with the best of the Sherpas: Nima, Dorjit, Cherma, Tenrit, Angdawa and young Pasang. As well as cutting steps, we're setting ropes and marker flags, to make what we've dubbed the "porters' highway"; this will allow the support party with the baggage to follow behind.

Cotterell hates hammering in pitons, he says it's spoiling the mountain with "blacksmiths' leavings". But Nima doesn't seem to mind, he tells me that what's important is not to treat the mountain with disrespect. "Never tell it bad word, Doctor Sahib. Never kick it in anger with feet."

The slope is steeper than it looked from below, and although not technically difficult, it turns out to be mostly ice, rather than snow. And this ice is *tough*, much tougher than in the Alps, so hacking each step is pretty stiff work. My heart is pounding, my throat sore from constant panting; and despite slathering on the Penaten, my face feels like cracked leather. But that's all *good*. It's what I want.

Pausing for breath, I push up my snow glasses. The glare is eye-watering, but just for a moment, I want to see things as they really are. Around me, the ice is fantastically sculpted, and glittering like white diamonds, with plunging shadows of astonishing sapphire. The air is achingly clear. I feel I could reach out and touch the guardian peaks.

"What are you grinning about?" pants Garrard below me.

"We're climbing the Crystal Mountain," I mumble through chapped lips.

"The what?"

Above us, Kits hoots with laughter. "Ignore him, Beak, he's mad!"

My laugh is a series of breathless gasps, but I can tell that Kits remembers. He loved that story as much as I did, although he'd never admit it now.

A while later, we pause in a patch of cerulean shade for a quick lunch of Mint Cake and Ginger Nuts, with vacuum flasks of tea. After that, I remain behind with the support party: that's Cotterell, Lobsang and the five remaining Sherpas.

Cotterell is very breathless, and will bear watching; I wonder if his extra years are starting to tell. But the Sherpas are amazing. It's beyond me how such small, slight people can climb with such enormous loads. I think Bauer's medical officer, Dr Hautmann, may be right, and there's something about their blood that allows them to tolerate oxygen depletion.

I certainly couldn't carry one of those packing crates, or a *doko* crammed with firewood. My rucksack can't weigh more than twenty pounds, but it feels like a ton. Every step is an effort, even though we're not really climbing, merely trudging up a steep slope. Digging in my crampons and gripping the head of my ice-axe like a walking stick, I jam in the shaft and haul myself up. And again. And again. But I'm grateful for the sheer, gasping drudgery. It banishes all sense of — well, of anything else.

100

Cedric is helping enormously. We'd just finished lunch when he came scrambling up, as I'd hoped he would, lashing his feathery tail and looking wildly pleased with himself for having found us.

The Sherpas leant on their ice-axes, grinning from ear to ear, and Cotterell struggled to look stern.

"We *can't* send him back now," I said. "If anything happened to him, it'd demoralise everyone!"

This made him smile. "So that's your argument, is it? A mascot, to encourage the troops?"

"Absolutely! He'll know when he's had enough, then the Sherpas can take him back to Base."

Cedric was glancing from me to Cotterell, clearly aware that we were talking about him.

"Oh, very well," growled Cotterell. "But he's your responsibility, Dr Pearce."

So that was settled. I've made Cedric a rope harness, criss-crossed over his back and around his forelegs, so that if he gets into trouble, we can haul him clear without throttling him. And I was right, he *has* lightened our spirits. He's amazingly sure-footed, and spends his time scrambling between the advance and support parties, having apparently conceived it his duty to ensure that none of us gets lost.

The climb after lunch wasn't quite as straightforward. We had to negotiate several tricky traverses of snow-filled crevasses, and giant blocks fallen from the cliffs. Then Pemba was hit in the thigh by a small icefall. Fortunately, it was only a bad bruise, but I'd just finished seeing to him when I glanced back, and saw someone far below, following us up the "porters' highway".

I told myself that McLellan must have sent a mail-runner from Base; but as we climbed higher, I kept an eye on the figure over my shoulder, and it was always there. Following.

At last, I checked with my field glasses — and it turned out to be a lump of ice. I was shaken by the intensity of my relief. What had I *imagined* it was?

By the time we'd struggled up the final stretch of the highway, the advance party had already pitched the tents at Camp One, and set the Primuses hissing under saucepans of ice, for tea.

Kits was bright-eyed with the sheer fun of the climb, and joshed us for arriving late. "The things you lot will do to avoid work!"

Camp One is on a broad balcony on the western flank of the Buttress. It's a cold, exposed, noisy camp, what with the canvas snapping and the wind roaring over the Saddle. But it's spacious, with several yards of level snow in front of the tents; and we're sheltered from avalanches by the top of the Buttress.

The support Sherpas headed off down the highway some time ago in order to reach Base before dark. First thing tomorrow, they'll start again with another load. Cotterell wants them shuttling between here and Base until we've amassed a sizeable stores dump, which we can use for establishing the upper camps.

From now on, we're doubling up in the tents, Kits sharing with Garrard, and I with Cotterell. I've left him

102

writing his journal in ours, and stepped out to catch the last of the light, and a few moments alone.

As soon as I'm beyond the lee of the tents, the wind cuts like a knife. Spindrift hisses at me, stiffening my windproofs as I trudge forwards to see how far we've climbed. I should have worn my balaclava. Within seconds, the wind snatches the heat from my face, and my skull is achingly cold. Wrapping my muffler around my head, I pull up my hood.

As I stand facing the tents, I crane my neck at a dizzying sweep of rock and ice that rises some seven thousand feet to Kangchenjunga West, one of the mountain's "lesser" peaks. To my right, the glaring chaos of the Upper Icefall is ablaze in the last of the sun. Somewhere over there is that crag. That's where we're heading tomorrow. Fortunately, it's out of sight behind the Buttress.

Turning my back on the tents, I trudge towards the edge of the "balcony". We've climbed higher than I thought. Staring down the snow slope makes me giddy. Far below, I can just make out the black hump of the knoll, and the Lyell graves.

I don't think I'll go any further. I'm pretty sure there's solid ice beneath me, but today we passed a good many cornices, their wind-blown snow cresting like enormous waves over thin air. Walk too far on one of those, and it might break, and send you hurtling into oblivion.

As I stare down the slope, that thought has a horrible fascination. If I fell . . .

When Kits and I were boys, we used to pester Aunt Ruth for the story of the Matterhorn disaster. We never tired of hearing it, and being bloodthirsty little brutes, we wanted details. Whymper's four companions had been roped together when they fell four thousand feet: striking the cliffs, then falling, then striking again. The impact stripped them naked and dismembered them. One man was identified only by his boot. Another by a rosary embedded in his jaw.

The sun dips behind the western peaks, and in the blink of an eye, the light on the snow has died. While my back was turned, clouds have closed in, and the tents are gone. Careful, Stephen. Head in the wrong direction now, and you're in trouble.

Very deliberately, I turn around one hundred and eighty degrees, and head for where I *think* the tents are.

Bit of a relief when they loom out of the fog. It certainly puts that business yesterday into perspective. Down at the lake, I scared myself silly. That makes me feel heartily ashamed. I saw a rock that resembled a man's head. Why did I let that put me in a funk?

The sheer *reality* of this mountain has done away with such nonsense. Charles Tennant was right to quote the Lepcha name for it: "the Big Stone". That's all Kangchenjunga is. But he wasn't right to be frightened of it. It might possess a semblance of animation, because of the wind, and the crack of canvas, and the distant rumble of an avalanche on the Saddle — but that's all it is, a *semblance*. *There is no life up here.* And no menace, either. The Sherpas are wrong. This mountain has no spirit, no sentience and no intent. It's not trying to kill us. It simply *is*.

Perhaps that's what we find frightening. Being on a mountain forces us to confront the vast, *un*sentient reality that's always present behind our own busy little human world, which we tuck around ourselves like a counterpane, to keep out the cold. No wonder that when we trespass into the mountains, we create phantoms. They're easier to bear than all this lifelessness.

Something nudges my thigh. It's Cedric, gazing up at me with warm, uncomprehending brown eyes.

Clumsily, with my mittened hand, I rub his ears. Time to go inside and get warm.

I've had enough immensity for one day.

CHAPTER
ELEVEN

Cocoa was ready by the time Cedric and I piled into
Garrard and Kits' tent, and dinner was steaming on the
second Primus. A tight squeeze, but at five degrees
below, it felt positively balmy, a comforting fug of damp
wool, paraffin, unwashed male and dog. The hiss of the
Primuses was loud, and everyone was coughing; up
here, sore throats are practically *de rigueur*.

No one was hungry — one isn't at altitude — but we
forced down porridge with dried apricots, plum jam
and shortbread. Meat didn't appeal, only sweet things,
although Cedric snuffled up a tin of sausages.

In the lurid yellow glow we looked like tramps: black
fingernails, matted hair and beards, leathery brown
faces. After we'd eaten, we sat in exhausted silence,
melting more snow and filling vacuum flasks for
early-morning tea. Then Cotterell and I returned to our
tent.

At altitude, everything takes ages. The smallest task
looms large. I've just spent half an hour unlacing my
gaiters and taking off my boots. Thank Heavens I had
the side opening of my sleeping bags sewn up; it's
much easier simply wriggling inside. Cotterell is still
fumbling with the buttons on his, and from the

adjacent tent, I can hear Garrard and Kits' noisy zip-fasteners, punctuated by swearing and coughs. The Sherpas' tent is silent as the grave; not even the sound of Nima's flute.

I lie with Cedric sprawled across my feet like a large, shaggy rug. He's a distraction from Cotterell, who occasionally stops breathing for an alarmingly long time. I'm doing it too. It's a minor symptom of mountain sickness called Cheyne-Stokes respiration. It's unpleasant having to struggle for breath, and even more unsettling when one hears someone else doing it.

Clicking on my electric torch, I check on Cotterell. Fast asleep, no bluish tinge around the lips. I switch off the torch, and darkness presses on my face like a hand.

Difficulty falling asleep is another minor symptom. I keep drifting off, only to be woken by palpitations. Even turning over makes my heart pound. We're at just under twenty thousand feet. Nearly nine thousand to go.

Buck up, Stephen, old man. Europeans can do this. Norton reached twenty-eight thousand on Everest. And last year that fellow with the monocle flew over the summit, and lived to tell the tale — and to make a rather too relentlessly cheery film.

I've pulled the drawstrings of my sleeping bags taut, with only my nose poking out. I used to hate that, but not any more. Snuggled inside two eiderdown sleeping bags, wearing my Shetland balaclava and my sheepskin motoring cap with the ear flaps tied under my chin, I'm practically deaf — and that's fine. I don't want to hear

Cotterell's breath cutting off. I don't want to be aware of the immensity outside.

"Our goal for today," Cotterell said at breakfast, "is to climb past the top of the Buttress, cross the Icefall, and establish Camp Two above the Crag."

Crossing the Icefall was exhausting. All morning we struggled through shadowy defiles and up rope ladders strung from pinnacles, until at last we emerged on to a vast, flat expanse of glaring snow at least half a mile wide. We were desperate for a rest, but we couldn't stop, for fear of avalanches.

Kits has just spotted an easy route to the Crag. He says it's scarcely an hour's climb. I'm relieved when I realise that this is the first time I've thought about the Crag since breakfast.

We've sent the Sherpas ahead, to cut steps on the final stretch, and we four sahibs are bringing up the rear, to do a spot of climbing on our own. Although one can't really call it climbing; we're simply following steps up an ice ridge the height of a ten-storey building, and the highway is marked with scarlet flags on bamboo poles. But we need them, as the weather's closing in.

Kits is leading, then Garrard, then me, and finally Cotterell. We're roped but not belayed, because as Kits says, "Running upstairs doesn't merit it."

Not quite running. The rasp of my breath is loud in my ears, and my ice-axe sends brittle shards skittering down the slope with that peculiar, shivering echo that always sounds slightly sinister. It's hypnotic, watching them spin and shatter on the Buttress a thousand feet below.

Much nearer, I hear Cotterell coughing, and the click of Cedric's claws. God knows how far that hound imagines he can follow us. Once we reach Camp Two, I'll have to send him back to Base, probably strapped in a Sherpa's basket, to prevent an escape.

The ridge is narrow, and on my right, that sudden drop to the Buttress keeps appearing and disappearing in the fog. Above me, Garrard and Kits are also doing a vanishing act. It's hard to tell them apart, both in their grey Grenfell cloth climbing suits with long tapes trailing from their hoods. They look scarcely human, their faces white with Penaten, their snow glasses turning them into blank-eyed ghouls.

Well, it *would* be hard to tell them apart, if it wasn't for Kits' inimitable style. It's been a few years since I climbed with him, and I'd forgotten just how good he is. He's a different man on a mountain. Gone is that puppyish boisterousness which at thirty-seven is beginning to seem a tad forced. He's utterly focused, and he has that indefinable sixth sense which climbers call "mountain feel". He moves differently, too, with a fluid, cat-like grace that Cotterell says reminds him of Mallory. I wouldn't know, I never had the luck to see Mallory climb. But watching Kits now, I feel an unexpected surge of family pride.

"It's not the way he moves that makes him such an amazing mountaineer," Garrard told me quietly, after breakfast. "It's the fact that you know, you absolutely know, that he'll never let you down."

He spoke with startling fervour, and I cast him a curious glance. His straggly blond beard only made his great beak stand out the more, and there was a glitter in his close-set eyes that made me wonder if his feelings for Kits mightn't run deeper than friendship. If that's true, I'm sorry for him. And I wonder if Kits knows.

Above me, Garrard seems to have drifted off course. It looks as if he's on the wrong side of the flags; although in this fog it's hard to be sure.

I'm squinting up at him when the snow beneath his right boot gives way with a *crump*, and takes him over the edge. He falls without a sound. No time to think. I drive in my ice-axe with all my strength, twist the rope around it to make a belay, and throw myself on the axe. A crack somewhere below, I hope to God that's Cotterell jamming in his axe. Another above, is that Kits digging in?

The wait can't be more than a second, but it feels like hours. Then my axe gives a shuddering jolt as it takes Garrard's full weight — and holds.

All this happens in an instant. There's a long, startled silence. The glassy clatter of falling ice. Then Garrard is clawing his way back. "Sorry, chaps! Sorry!"

I'm becoming aware that my ice-axe has given me a painful bruise in the abdomen, and that Cotterell has climbed up and is clapping me on the back. "Good show, Dr Pearce, jolly good show!" Now the three of us are grinning and pawing each other with relief, and Cedric is barking and trying to lick the Penaten off our faces.

"What's going on down there?" shouts Kits, just visible through the fog. "I heard a crack — "

"Missed my step!" yells Garrard. "Bit of a near thing!"

"Christ, Beak, are you all right?" Kits' face is sharp with concern, and Garrard flushes with pleasure. "Fine! Feel like a bloody fool!"

Kits breaks into a grin. "Bloody fool is right! Next time, watch where you're going!"

"I know, I'm an idiot! If it wasn't for Stephen, we'd have had it!"

Kits' grin freezes. "Well done, Stephen." Do I imagine that forced note? Surely he can't be jealous?

Before we set off again, I give Garrard a quick checking-over. The rope has given him some burns and a badly bruised midriff (he's lucky it didn't break his ribs), and he's rather more shaken than he cares to admit.

We all are. It happened so fast, and it only took one small mistake. It always does. We know that, we've heard the stories: the dropped mitten, the piton inadvertently hammered into rotten ice . . . But it's different when it happens to you. It makes you realise as never before that on a mountain, what matters is your fellow climbers.

Except that's not true, what's even more important is blind chance. If the rope between Garrard and Kits hadn't happened to be considerably longer than that between me and Garrard, his fall would have pulled Kits off the mountain, too. Then either the rope would have snapped under the weight of two men, or my ice-axe would have given way, and we'd all have been finished.

Everyone is relieved to have reached Camp Two. Despite our plans, it's on the same site as Lyell's — in other words, right under the Crag. We've arrived too late in the day to camp above it; and Kits' objections to the site, which were so strong down on the grave knoll, have melted away. That's probably because Cotterell thinks the Crag, which is a good hundred feet high, will provide shelter from avalanches; and whatever Cotterell says is good enough for Kits.

I'm too exhausted to care. Garrard's "near thing" has put all that into perspective. Whatever I saw down at Base feels a hundred years ago. It doesn't *matter*. What matters is the fellows I'm with, and the knowledge that if *I* have a near thing, I can count on them — as they can count on me.

Camp Two is even windier than Camp One, and unpleasantly cramped, with only a couple of yards in front of the tents before a sudden drop to the Buttress. To my left, as I stand facing camp, the end of the Crag overhangs that zigzag crevasse I spotted from the knoll. Luckily, though, we didn't have to cross it on our way here, but found a way around.

How strange to be on such a narrow ledge, surrounded by all this space. At times, the clouds close in and I can't see a thing, and that's alarming, as I can still sense the emptiness around. Then the clouds rip apart and suddenly there's that horrifying drop, and above me the no less horrifying heights. The shifts

112

between seeing and not seeing are so abrupt, so silent . . . It's disorientating.

Lobsang and the other Sherpas have headed back down the highway to Camp One, but Tenrit, Cherma, Angdawa, Dorjit, Pasang and the indefatigable Nima are huddled in their tent, heating *tsampa* on their Primus. These people amaze me. Apart from a few bumps and bruises, they're fighting fit.

It's my turn and Cotterell's to play host in our tent, and we dine on fairly disgusting pemmican soup with powdered egg, Mint Cake and tapioca pudding laced with treacle and lime pickle (that's my idea, for Vitamin C). We wash it down with Cotterell's special brew: bulls-eyes dissolved in Horlick's "Malted Milk". It's perfect for dunking Digestive biscuits, and fast becoming a favourite. God knows what it's doing to our teeth.

We're still a bit overwrought after Garrard's mishap, and all talking at once.

"If the weather holds, we should be able to make the Great Shelf in two or three days . . ."

"Cedric, out of the *way* . . ."

"Frankly, I'd prefer to do without bottled oxygen, I don't think it's playing fair. And those masks make one feel so frightfully cut off . . ."

"Yes, but it helped them on Everest — "

"Well, Bauer thinks it's weakening."

"He's German," says Kits, "they think everything's weakening." That makes everyone laugh.

"What do you think, Dr Pearce?" asks Cotterell.

I smile. "Afraid I'm with Bauer. I wouldn't want to rely on it. Although I'd keep a few canisters for a bracer at night."

After that, we veer off into the hoary old question of why one climbs. Cotterell mentions McLellan and his God. Garrard pulls his beak in embarrassment and mumbles something about John Ruskin and beauty. I say that I like the sheer pointlessness of it: the pure endeavour for endeavour's sake.

Kits rolls his eyes at me in affectionate exasperation, which isn't affectionate at all. "For Heaven's *sake*, Bodge, it's a *mountain*! Why can't you simply climb it, and to hell with why?"

"But Kits, that's exactly what I mean."

He flushes. "Well I don't think it does to talk about these things. One ought simply to work it out for oneself, and keep quiet!"

Garrard shoots me a wry glance, and Cotterell smoothes things over by doling out the last of the biscuits.

Kits is miffed because Garrard's near thing has brought me into the fold. He'd rather keep me on the outside of the cosy little *coterie* he's formed with Garrard and Cotterell. It makes me wonder what he said about me before I joined them in Darjeeling.

The talk has turned stilted, so I start checking everyone's pulse. Unsurprisingly, given that we're at just under twenty-two thousand feet, we're all rather feeling it. Garrard has a touch of sciatica, Kits' right hand is frost-nipped, and Cotterell has taken a chill in the kidneys; although he won't admit it, he's clearly

114

feeling grim. He swears by his asthma cigarettes and a red flannel body belt that saw him through the trenches, but I'll need to keep an eye on him — tactfully, as he's sensitive about his age.

Once the others have returned to their tent, and he's in his sleeping bag, I improvise a hot-water bottle with spare rubber tubing from the oxygen apparatus. He says it's grand and he's feeling better already, but I'm not convinced.

I'm lying on my side, facing him, with Cedric between me and the icy tent wall. The wind is flinging snow at the tent; it sounds like gravel, and there's that never-ending bang of canvas. I'm exhausted, but too excited to sleep.

I'm beginning to realise that I haven't run away from my life, I've *found* it. Studying medicine is the one thing I've ever done that has had nothing to do with Kits; but until now, I've never understood how much that means. And this is *real* doctoring: a million miles from pressing the plump hands of Knightsbridge matrons.

There's so much I want to learn, too. *Why* do Sherpas tolerate altitude better than Europeans? Do they adapt, or is it inherited? Why shouldn't *I* be the one to find out?

Besides, I *like* these people, and they could do with a good doctor. In the foothills, we passed several villages full of friendly, filthy peasants. I came across lots of inflamed eyes and chest infections, and I did what I could with those supplies I could spare, but there's so much more I could do.

115

When all this is over, why shouldn't I stay on in India, or Nepal or Sikkim?

I'm awake in an instant. Something's wrong. A sound woke me, but now it's stopped. I've no idea what it was, only that I'm afraid. I'm huddled on my side with my knees drawn up to my chest. My scalp is crawling, my breathing fast and shallow. Why? What does my body know that I don't?

Around me, camp is silent and still. No wind, no snores from the other tents. It wasn't a nightmare that woke me, or an avalanche; I can't hear the rumble of débris. And I am truly awake: I can feel my fingernails digging into my palms, and the bristles of my beard as I bite my lower lip. I'm cold, so cold. A few inches in front of me, I make out Cotterell's heaving bulk, but there's no Cedric at my back, just freezing canvas bulging inwards with the weight of snow.

All this flashes through my mind in a heartbeat as I stare into the dark, too frightened to move.

Dimly, by contrast, I make out the canvas sucking in and out, and the grey snow driving past the celluloid window in the front flap at my feet. It comes to me in an icy wash of terror that I can't hear any of it. No wind, no snapping canvas, no gravelly snow, not even Cotterell breathing. Only my own panicky breath. Reality has sucked back like a tide, leaving me trapped behind a wall of silence.

The next moment, with appalling certainty, I *know*. There's something outside the tent.

116

I'm desperate to wake Cotterell, but I can't. I dare not put out my hand, dare not move. And now I hear — or rather, I sense within the silence — that something is coming up behind me.

The crunch of footsteps on snow crust: a dragging, halting gait — no, not a gait; it sounds . . . it sounds as if it's on all fours.

If I sat upright and peered through the window . . . But I can't. I can't bear the thought of what I might see.

Now I hear the rustle and creak of frozen windproofs. It's rising to its feet. Much closer, right behind me. Only a thin layer of canvas between us.

The rustling stops. The stillness is appalling.

I force myself to twist round and peer at the front flap.

My heart jerks. There's a head in the window. Motionless. Close. And yet, no haze of frosty breath. It was behind me and now it's there.

I can't move. My limbs are frozen, as if caked in ice. I can't bear to look for another second. I screw my eyes shut. When I open them, it's gone.

Like the snapping of a spell, I can hear the wind and the bang-bang of canvas; and Cotterell's stertorous breath.

I can move. I struggle out of my sleeping bags and drag on wind jacket, windproof trousers, boots. I fumble for my electric torch, but don't dare light it. I pull on my undergloves, shove my mittens in my pockets with the torch, grapple with the tent flaps' frozen slipknots. My heart is hammering against my ribs, but I don't hesitate. I have to know.

The sky is black. No moon; a scattering of stars in the rents between clouds. Dim grey snow hissing across camp. There's nothing by the tent.

Crawling outside, I lurch to my feet. I take a few steps to make sure.

The crackle of frozen canvas, then a shaft of yellow light stabs the snow.

"Stephen?" Kits' head pokes out between the flaps in a smoky haze of breath. "What are you doing?" he whispers.

Clicking on my torch, I sweep the ground around my tent. The snow is pristine. No footprints. Only my own few faltering steps.

I switch off my torch and scan the camp, my eyes sweeping the tents, the grey mounds of the stores dump, up towards —

It's on the Crag. Dark against the stars and horribly *there*: a hooded figure in climbing gear.

Until this moment, I could have persuaded myself that it was a dream, but not now, standing here with Kits behind me and the wind flinging snow in my face like glass.

"Stephen! What's wrong?"

I glance at him over my shoulder, then back to the Crag. The figure is gone. But it was there. I saw it. Kits didn't. Only me.

I clear my throat. "Nothing," I croak. "Nothing's wrong."

CHAPTER
TWELVE

It can't have been an hallucination caused by mountain sickness. I'm hardly suffering from that; just a touch of nausea and breathlessness, and they're minor symptoms.

If I'd fought in Flanders like Cotterell, I could put it down to war-strain. Repressed experiences thrusting up from my unconscious mind. But I'm not "repressing" anything. I *heard* those noises outside the tent. I didn't imagine them, and it wasn't a dream. There's a reason I pulled on my clothes and crawled out into the cold: because I *heard* something.

And I saw what I saw on the Crag.

But what *was* it?

I'm amazed that at breakfast, nothing shows in my face. The four of us are crammed into Garrard and Kits' tent, and no one notices a thing.

Kits asks through a mouthful of porridge why I was outside in the dark, and I tell him I'd returned from relieving myself and was looking for Cedric. Casually, I ask if he saw anything odd.

"Odd? What d'you mean?"

"On the Crag. I thought . . . Looked like a *gorak*. Pretty rum, spotting a bird this high. You didn't see it?"

He chuckles. "No, but that's obviously what roused Cedric. He's a devil for *goraks*, aren't you, my lad? Lucky for him he found his way back to my tent!"

So now there's no room for doubt. Kits didn't see it. Only me. And I can't tell anyone, they'd think it's the altitude and send me back to Base.

Nearly five and getting light, but it's snowing too hard to make a start, so we're stuck here in Camp Two. Cotterell is writing in our tent, and I'm with Garrard and Kits. The more cramped it is, the safer I feel.

Garrard is reading, and Cedric is sprawled across his legs with his muzzle between his paws, casting me sheepish glances — as well he might, after deserting me last night. Kits and I are taking turns to peer through the window. He's as desperate as I am to leave, although with him it's because he's easily bored and detests inaction.

"I *think* it's clearing up," he says hopefully.

"Nima doesn't think it'll last," I add.

Garrard snorts. "Be realistic, chaps, it's a white-out!"

He's right. What if it goes on all day? I don't know what I'll do if we have to stay here another night.

It's no good, I have to face the truth. There's something terribly wrong with Camp Two.

What do I mean by "wrong"? Well I don't mean ghosts. Not in the sense of disembodied spirits; I don't believe in them. As a scientist, of course, I'm prepared to accept evidence to the contrary, but so far I haven't come across any. And what I experienced last night is *not* evidence to the contrary. No. When the last synapse in the brain flickers and dies, that's it, lights out. That is what I believe.

But *energy*, now. Energy can be neither created nor destroyed, so isn't it at least *possible* that some kind of energy — perhaps magnetic, or even some force of emotion — may have lingered here for years? And perhaps — *perhaps* there's something about me that makes me a sort of "physical medium" for that energy: like a battery, or a lightning rod? Maybe that's what Cedric sensed last night. Maybe that's why he still won't come near me.

It's an hypothesis, and it makes me feel slightly better. I've put a frame around the "wrongness". I've contained it.

And this means that there's really no *point* in trying to learn any more about what happened to Lyell and his companions. It won't change a thing. What I need to hold on to is the fact that whatever is wrong with Camp Two affects *only* Camp Two. That's crucial. I had no sense of "wrongness" on the climb up from the grave knoll, or at Camp One, or on the climb to Camp Two itself.

Then why is it so strong here?

Well, it must be because this is where Lyell pitched *his* Camp Two. And presumably, too, because somewhere above us is the place where that first accident happened, the one that turned their luck. How did Cotterell's book put it? *They had climbed to a little over twenty-two thousand feet when, as often happens at altitude, a trivial error triggered disaster.*

But that's *above* us. So why is the wrongness *here*?

"Stephen?" Kits is holding out a steaming mug of tea.

"Thanks. What's the weather doing?"

He pulls a face. "Still, it's not even nine o'clock. Plenty of time to clear up."

"Ever the optimist," murmurs Garrard without raising his eyes from his book.

The tea is sweet and strong and marvellously bracing, but while I sit drinking and chatting, the animal part of me remains watchful and tense. What I experienced last night has set me apart. Even now, in this cramped little tent, I'm bracing myself — because at any moment, another crack might open up, and the darkness seep through.

I was wrong, I can't go on like this. It's not knowing that makes it so dreadful. Come on, Stephen, no more denial. The key to all this must be in the Lyell expedition. You really do need to know.

"Kits," I say briskly. "*Bloody But Unbowed*. Did you bring it with you?"

Time passes unevenly at altitude. An hour goes by in a minute, and a minute stretches to an hour. Today has felt like a year.

Still snowing. Dense grey billows swirling past the window. *Bloody But Unbowed* lies unopened on my rucksack. I can't bring myself to read it just yet, so instead I head out to check on the Sherpas.

The wind is a granite fist in my face as I stagger forwards, clutching the rope that's strung between the tents. I keep my head down, and refuse to look up at

122

the Crag. I experience nothing untoward, but the sense that I *might* — the dread like a stone in the pit of my stomach — is almost as bad.

The Sherpas respectfully make room for me and hand me a mug of tea. Nima says the snow will be over by morning, although I suspect that's wishful thinking: he hates this camp as much as I. He says it's unlucky; that's why Cherma has frostnip. I tell him Cherma has frostnip because yesterday he took off his mittens too often. Nima nods politely, but I can see he's not convinced. Cherma gives a gap-toothed grin and says it doesn't hurt much. As I dose him with aspirin, I tell him that it's when it doesn't hurt that he needs to worry.

It's four in the afternoon and I'm back in our tent. Back with *Bloody But Unbowed* on my rucksack, waiting to be read. Cedric is with Garrard and Kits, and Cotterell is dozing. His colour is good and he's breathing more freely, but I plan to use him as an excuse to sit up tonight with an electric lamp. I've no intention of going to sleep. I don't dare.

Still snowing, still windy. The endless snap of canvas is horribly wearing on the nerves.

At lunch, to keep up our spirits, we discussed the site for Camp Three. We aim to pitch it more or less where Lyell did, at the foot of a cliff on the eastern edge of the Icefall, within a day's climb of the Great Shelf. Cotterell said the plan for Camp Three is to dig ice caves; apparently Bauer found them warmer than tents, and safe from avalanches. "And no bloody noise," Garrard added wearily.

At first, I didn't care for the idea: an ice cave sounds unpleasantly like a snow globe. But on reflection, I like the sound of those solid walls. There'd be no chance of anything coming up behind me.

So now, Lyell.

To my annoyance, my heart starts to pound as I open Kits' much-thumbed, heavily annotated little volume. I can't bring myself to dive straight in at the point where they establish Camp Two, so instead, I skim the opening chapters.

The first surprise is that I can't stand Lyell. I was a boy of nine when I last read *Bloody But Unbowed*, and at that age, I worshipped him: *a soldier tempered by the suns of the Punjab and the grim task of tackling the Boer in the South African War.* I wanted to *be* him. I longed to follow in his footsteps and take a nonchalant "stroll" across a twenty-thousand-foot pass in the Karakorams. (He wrote a book about that too, *Jaunts in the Karakoram-Himalaya*, which I also lapped up.) What I admired most was that he never seemed to *try.* In the Karakorams, he didn't even bother taking an ice-axe or nailed boots, *merely a certain amount of pluck.*

Reading him now, all this strikes me as the height of arrogance. To Lyell, amateurism is a mark of breeding. He's a snob of the first water. His contempt for *the stench of professionalism* drips from every page. He even sneers at crampons (he calls them "climbing irons") as being unsporting and bad form. No wonder the expedition was plagued by what he refers to as "mishaps": stolen rations, supply problems, coolie mutinies.

Oddly enough, he seems to loathe Kangchenjunga itself. He feels neither awe nor curiosity, he simply wishes to conquer: *It is an affront, a challenge to Man's supremacy.*

As a leader, he's a tyrant, sounding a *reveille* every morning on an alpine horn (I wonder how his fellow sahibs enjoyed that!). And he regards his coolies as barely sentient brutes: *vicious and disgustingly prolific, their hovels swarm with progeny like weevils in mouldy rice.* He sees nothing wrong in making them trek the glacier in bare feet, and when one of them collapses and begs to be left to die, Lyell is *happy to comply*, merely begrudging the dying man's kin the time it takes to say a prayer and cover his face with a kerchief.

What strikes me most forcibly is his overweening vanity. His fellow sahibs are mere cyphers, sketchily described. This expedition is all about Edmund Lyell.

But I'm prevaricating. The climb. What about the climb?

All seems to have gone well up to Camp Two, barring the odd "scrape" — in which Lyell, of course, usually saves the day. The chapter after that is headed "A Fatal Blunder".

After a splendid night and a hearty breakfast of meat lozenges and Brand's peptone soup, we set off from Camp Two in excellent spirits. With the baggage coolies bringing up the rear, we spent an agreeable morning engaged in some tolerably tricky climbing, our aim being to conquer the formidable ice crag which reared like a wild beast over Camp Two. This we accomplished around noon, and paused atop it for a spot of luncheon. That was when disaster struck.

"Stephen?" shouts Kits from his tent. "You haven't forgotten that it's our turn to cook dinner?"

"Um . . ." I croak. "In a minute."

It all began on the Crag. Of course it did. Here at Camp Two, we're at twenty-one thousand nine hundred feet. Cotterell's little book said that it was at just over twenty-two thousand that things went wrong.

We had taken off our rück-sacks in order to avail ourselves of our water-bottles, Lyell goes on. Ward, as was his custom, had seated himself apart from the rest of us. He must have made some clumsy move and knocked his rück-sack off the edge, although the first we knew of it was when we heard him shout, "Below!" as a warning to the baggage coolies, who were still climbing.

Ward? Who on earth is Ward?

Afterwards, we surmised that his rück-sack must have snagged a few feet down, thus tempting him to further foolishness — although none of us saw this, as it happened too quickly. What we do know is that instead of soliciting our help, Ward then compounded his error by trying to retrieve the article alone. The reader may imagine our consternation when we saw him climbing unroped a few feet down the crag, in an idiotic attempt to reach for his rück-sack! He contrived to seize it in one hand, then lost his balance and fell. He made no sound — men seldom do when they fall — and he struck the ice with a sickening crunch a hundred feet below, on the edge of the crevasse. He did not respond to our calls and we feared the worst, but I conceived it my duty to climb down and ascertain his condition. This I did, ably belayed by Tennant, and on reaching the fallen man, I found my melancholy supposition confirmed.

"Come on, Stephen, no shirking!"
"I said I'm coming!"

He was quite dead, having apparently broken his neck, but as the body was half overhanging the crevasse, I saw at once that it would be too hazardous to attempt to retrieve it alone. Accordingly, I climbed back to the others, then sent a runner down to the baggage train with orders for four coolies to remain behind and recover the body. Thereafter, we five said a brief prayer for our fallen comrade, then steeled ourselves to the grim task of continuing our ascent to the Great Shelf.

The reader who lacks mountain experience may regard such behaviour as callous. The seasoned alpinist will, I trust, sympathise with our predicament. The afternoon was wearing on and we were driven by a harsh imperative, namely, the absolute necessity of establishing the next camp before darkness fell.

Feverishly, I flick through the remaining pages. Lyell's account of the rest of the climb doesn't seem to

127

differ from the outline in Cotterell's book. Soon after that fatal fall from the Crag, a blizzard drove everyone back to Camp Two, and kept them there for three days. By the time the weather cleared, they were so weakened by the "rarefied air" that they had no choice but to abandon the attempt on the summit. Shortly afterwards, as they were making their descent to Camp One, the avalanche struck.

When I was a boy, the avalanche was my favourite part of the story, but reading Lyell now, I find it nauseating. He makes it sound as if he and Tennant managed the rescue practically single-handed: digging their comrades from the snow, raising a cairn on the knoll for Freemantle and Knight, bearing the injured Stratton and Yates back over the Yalung. There's scarcely a line about the *two hundred coolies* who did the actual work. Or the four coolies who also lost their lives in the avalanche.

And as far as I can tell, there's no further mention of Ward. Who the bloody hell *was* Ward?

"Where's Pache, and who's Ward?" I ask Kits a few minutes later, as I open a tin of sausages to add to the porridge.

Kits is miffed at me and doesn't reply.

I repeat the question.

"What?" he says irritably.

"Who's Ward?"

"He was the first man to die, the one who dropped the rucksack. Cedric, *down!*"

"I thought that was Pache."

"Oh Stephen, *really*! Pache belonged to a completely different expedition!"

I stare at him. "What?"

Crossly, he stirs the porridge, narrowing his eyes against the steam. "Lieutenant Alexis Pache, a Swiss-German, killed with three coolies in an avalanche on the expedition led by that scoundrel Crowley in '05. *1905*, Stephen, the year *before* Lyell! As you'd have known if you'd bothered to pay your respects at the poor fellow's grave."

I've cut myself on the tin. Blood is oozing from a gash in the heel of my hand. "So — where's Ward buried?"

Kits spoons dried vegetables into the porridge. "He isn't."

"But . . . Lyell retrieved the body. He said that."

"You didn't read very attentively, did you? Lyell ordered the coolies to retrieve the body, but they disobeyed. Then, after the blizzard, Lyell searched, but he couldn't find it."

My heart is flopping about like a landed fish. "Then what happened to it?"

"God knows. Blown off the mountain, down the crevasse. It was gone, that's all anyone knows. Rest in peace, Arthur Ward."

CHAPTER
THIRTEEN

He didn't have a middle name; he was just plain Arthur Ward. And according to Lyell, nobody liked him. He was an engraver "by trade" (one can almost smell Lyell's disdain), and he didn't smoke, drink or chat. In short, he wasn't *clubbable*. Beyond that, I can't find much about him in *Bloody But Unbowed*.

Cotterell groans in his sleep. He vomited after dinner, so my excuse for staying awake has become reality. I'm sitting with my back to him, because I can't bear to have the wall of the tent behind me. So far, I've heard nothing untoward. Only the creak of canvas and the spatter of snow.

Arthur Ward seems to have been a last-minute replacement, like me. He's not in any of the photographs, and Lyell doesn't describe him, so he has no face. From what I can glean, he was a talented climber, and they tolerated him, but they didn't care to be shown up. Once, Ward saved Tennant's life when he was stunned by falling ice. He was sliding towards a crevasse, and Ward grabbed him by the strap of his rucksack and hauled him to safety. Lyell only sees fit to mention this *en passant*.

And later, he inveighs against climbers who aren't gentlemen; he clearly means Ward. *There is a breed of man which sees nothing dishonourable in the use of "climbing aids". Such men can make tolerable alpinists, but they invariably betray themselves with the impulsiveness and lack of nerve inherent in their class.*

So there we are. Ward was common, talented, and didn't fit in. That's all I have. That, and the fact that this place where I am now — or to be precise, two hundred yards off on the edge of the crevasse — is where, twenty-nine years ago, Arthur Ward broke his neck in the kind of stupid, hypoxic accident that kills so many mountaineers.

Is that why Camp Two is haunted? Did his death leave some sort of "psychic imprint"? Some lingering energy that re-enacts the accident whenever an attuned individual happens along? And I do believe that it is a re-enactment. I haven't forgotten that cry of "*Below!*" which woke me at Base.

But none of this feels enough to justify what's happening. Ward's death was violent and unnecessary, but that's hardly unusual, it's how climbers die. So why him? Why not Freemantle or Knight, or Lieutenant Pache from '05, or one of the porters, or that solitary American in '29, or one of Bauer's lot from the north face? Why am I so convinced that it's Ward?

Because — because none of the others died *here*. And because that figure I saw on the Crag wasn't a Sherpa, but a European.

And because I feel it.

Cotterell wakes with a moan, and bursts into a fit of coughing. When it's over, I make him gargle with dilute Condy's fluid, and give him a chlorate of potash tablet. I ask him how he feels.

"On the mend," he mumbles. I doubt that. His grey eyes are bloodshot, and with his grizzled beard, he looks crumpled and old.

He heaves a ragged sigh. "I wish I could get rid of these damned images."

My heart skips a beat. "Images?"

"Flashes, really. Nonsense. But rather ghastly."

"In what way?"

"Oh, they seem to sort of — *come* at me. Doesn't matter what I'm doing. Climbing, eating, trying to sleep. Can't keep em away."

"How long has this been going on?"

"Um — well, since we started the climb."

All this time? "What sort of images?"

He blinks. "Faces, mostly."

"Whose?"

To my consternation, his throat works, and his eyes grow moist. "I can't . . ."

"I'm sorry, Major, I didn't mean to pry — "

"No no, it's . . ." He pinches the bridge of his nose and scowls. "He was my subaltern. When we found him, he — we identified him by his cigarette case."

My disappointment is so savage that it elbows out sympathy. I didn't want it to be the War, I wanted him to have seen what I've seen. Then I wouldn't be alone.

I pour us both a tot of brandy, and he sips gratefully. "I don't *understand* why I only see him," he mutters. "I mean, one saw a good deal of — that. One became rather blasé." He scratches his hairline, which is already raw. "You don't think I — I mean, there's never been anything *wrong* in my family. I can't be — unstrung, or what-have-you?"

"You mean, mad?"

Sometimes, merely saying the word is a kind of exorcism. I can see the tension draining out of him.

"No, I don't think you're mad. Chaps with war neurosis mostly have some kind of bad blood in the family. There are lots of fellows like you, who simply have nightmares. These days, we call it war-strain."

"Ah. You don't say."

His ignorance astounds me. Has the poor chap been carrying this alone all these years? Or is the mountain bringing it out? I won't ask, he's clearly embarrassed at having let down his guard.

As a distraction for us both, I check him over. Heart rate and breathing sound, no water on the lungs.

We don't speak again. Cotterell pretends to fall asleep, and I try to push snow off the sagging tent. The canvas feels as if it's resisting me.

Poor old Cotterell. Well, there's no bad blood in my family either and I'm pretty sure I'm not going mad, but right now, that's not much comfort. It's two in the morning: another two hours before we can think about getting ready to head off — *if* it stops snowing. And then we'll be climbing the Crag, where Ward was killed. What if I see something? What if I panic and kill myself, or someone else?

One thing's for sure. Even if this snow keeps up, I am *not* spending another night in this camp. I shall declare that in my medical opinion, Cotterell must descend to Camp One, and I must go with him. Or something. This is the last night I will ever spend at Camp Two.

Nima was right, the weather did clear. There's not a cloud in the sky. The snowstorm has buried Camp Two, and we've left Tenrit and Dorjit digging out the tents and the stores.

Our aim today is to climb the Crag and head up the edge of the Icefall, establishing Camp Three about a thousand feet below the Great Shelf, on a sort of plateau beneath the ice cliff. We've found a tolerable route up the Crag, thank God, and it isn't technically difficult; Kits says that won't come until after the Great Shelf.

Cutting steps is the usual exhausting toil, and the sun's so fierce I have to peel off sweater, muffler and mittens. Then clouds seep down and I have to put it all on again — and at this altitude, it takes *ages*, and one must be so dreadfully careful. I'm trying not to think about Ward dropping his rucksack. Perhaps the others are too, for it's been three hours and we've climbed in total silence. No humming from Nima or Pasang, no whistling from Garrard or Kits. Even Cedric seems cowed.

When you've been frightened — I mean really frightened, as I have — you don't relax afterwards. All through the snowstorm, and now today, I've been braced, in case the threat hasn't passed. It's as if there's another self inside me, keeping watch.

We're nearly at the top of the Crag, where Ward met his death. What an ugly phrase that is, evoking an image of a shrouded grey figure, from whom there is no escape.

A shadow slides across me and I duck. It's a bloody *gorak*, of all things.

Garrard, above me, glances down with a lopsided grin. "Seems our camp follower has joined us from Base."

"How d'you know it's the same one?" I pant.

"I don't, but it feels appropriate. Poe, and all that."

With an indignant *whuff*, Cedric scrambles after the bird, which hitches itself on to the wind. The dog can't stop in time, and nearly pitches off the Crag. We yell at him to come back, and he slithers down to us, lashing his feathery tail.

That's broken the tension; even Cotterell's chuckling. Soon afterwards, we reach the top of the Crag.

It hasn't quite finished with us. It turns out that the crevasse, which I thought we'd left down at Camp Two, actually zigzags up and *behind* the Crag. It now lies directly across our path.

At its narrowest, it's about six feet across. Icicles a yard long hang from its edge, leading the eye down into fathomless black.

I'm the last man on the rope, so I'll be the last to cross. Kits has already clipped together the ladder that Nima's been carrying, and has bridged that yawning gap. He goes first (of course): not crawling, but walking.

"Nothing to it!" he calls when he's on the other side. Thanks, I think sourly. That helps a lot.

Garrard takes the ladder at a cautious crawl, as does Cotterell. Like all of us, he's roped by the waist. He stares ahead without looking down.

Once he's across, he grins at me. "Reminds me of the duckboards in Flanders!" There's a touch of bravado about him. He's telling me to forget all that guff about faces last night.

Nima and Pasang are next, then it's my turn. I'm not scared, just reluctant. According to Lyell, Ward landed with a "sickening crunch", and lay half over the crevasse. Of course, that would have been over the part of the crevasse that is *below* the Crag. But it's still the same crevasse.

Nima carries Cedric in his *doko*, and tackles the ladder at a sure-footed walk, so that the dog has no time to be alarmed. Pasang also walks across, singing a tuneless prayer under his breath.

Now the five of them are waiting for me on the other side. A veil of wind-blown snow drifts between us, shrouding them in white. With their snow glasses and Penaten-smeared faces, they seem scarcely human.

"Come on, Stephen," barks Kits. "Chop-chop!"

Gripping my ice-axe in one hand, I crawl on to the ladder. It sags under me. I *won't* look down at what yawns beneath, but I feel its pull.

I keep going, fixing my eyes on the others — and for the blink of an eye, there seem to be *six* men watching me, not five. I count them. Kits, Garrard, Cotterell, Nima, Pasang. That's *five*, you idiot. Get a grip.

"What's the matter, Bodge!" taunts Kits. "Got the wind up?"

Behind me, ice falls with a glassy tinkle, and without thinking, I glance down. Deep in the blackness, I fancy that something moves. Is Ward's body down there? Is that why it haunts?

"Nearly there, you duffer!" Kits is stretching out his hand, and there's a reassuring note in his voice that I don't like. It's as if he's cajoling a frightened horse. Or a younger brother who's never quite measured up.

Ignoring his hand, I reach the edge, and lurch to my feet. As long as he doesn't come out with one of his snide little "jokes" about Bodge nearly flunking it.

Instead, he pushes up his snow glasses and give me a pitying look, then turns away.

And just for a moment, I hate him.

The weather is glorious, and so is Camp Three — chiefly because it isn't Camp Two. We can no longer even *see* Camp Two, or the Crag, or that bloody crevasse. We're at twenty-two thousand eight hundred feet, and we've left it all behind.

We've pitched Camp Three where Lyell did, at the foot of the ice cliff. It's windy, as we're facing west, but much roomier than Camp Two, with none of that alarming feeling of huddling on a ledge. The site is enlivened by the odd enormous block of ice, and so level that we don't need crampons. In fact, the snow is too soft; it would only ball up underneath, and make them dangerous.

The tents have been pitched at the foot of the cliff, and in front there's a good twenty yards of flattish snow — we've dubbed it the Plateau — before a nasty drop to the Yalung Glacier. As one stands facing camp, the stockpile and latrine area are to one's left, and some way beyond them is another crevasse — but it's not *the* crevasse, so I don't mind. Anyway, we can't see it from the tents, because of the stockpile.

Last night, the temperature dropped to forty below. That roaring wind, which sounded so distant down at Base, was much louder up here — and yet I slept better than I have since we started the climb. No doubt that's sheer exhaustion, and relief at having escaped Camp Two.

I woke to find my eyelashes frozen shut, and the tent and my sleeping bag crackling with frost. We'd declared a non-climbing day, but camp was in shadow, and we couldn't get warm — until mid-morning, when the sun reached us, and within ten minutes we were *baking*, and strolling about in shirtsleeves.

Tenrit and Cherma have gone down to Camp Two to finish excavating the last of the stores, and the rest of us are in camp. Another day's climbing should take us to the Great Shelf, where we'll establish Camp Four. From there, it can't be more than two days to the summit. However, the plan is to stay here for a few days, to stockpile supplies and get out of this wind by digging the famous ice caves out of the foot of the cliff. I'm glad. I like it here.

Kits and I are working on one cave, Cotterell and Garrard tackling the other "next door", and the

138

Sherpas are beavering away at the third. It's my turn to dig, which means I'm lying on my back, hacking as best I can with my ice-axe a few inches above my face, while Kits crouches behind me, shovelling away débris with a saucepan.

Under any conditions, this would be tiring. At nearly twenty-three thousand feet, it's sheer bloody hell. But it's a simple, *physical* hell, and I find it bizarrely enjoyable. Ice chips are showering down and soaking me to the skin, and when I pause for breath, my arms are shaking with fatigue.

From next door, Garrard gives a muffled groan. "How the blazes did those Huns manage a cave big enough for *six* men?"

"That's what they *say* they did," Cotterell mutters darkly.

"Remind me again," I pant. "Why are we doing this?"

"Because it's fun," replies Kits.

We exchange grins, and quote Aunt Ruth in unison: *"And what can't be avoided had better be enjoyed!"*

Suddenly we're spluttering with laughter, and Kits is bombarding me with frozen slush. I scramble out and pelt him with snowballs, and Cedric is barking at us and the snow is glittering and we're *happy*, like that time when we were boys and freewheeling down Primrose Hill, and everything felt just *right*.

Last night we slept in the tents again, as the ice caves won't be finished for another day at least. I was so shattered I didn't wake once.

Lots to do today. In between bouts of digging, one has to dry one's gear in the sun, prepare food, and melt snow for endless mugs of tea. Garrard has devised a clever short cut for that: you fill a wind jacket with snow and set it to melt in the sun, collecting the water in a canvas bucket. It saves effort *and* paraffin; even if the water does taste of canvas.

All this sounds remarkably orderly, but we can't forget that altitude plays tricks. Yesterday evening, I was about to wriggle into my sleeping bag when I was surprised to find Garrard's brass altimeter lying on top. I'd borrowed it earlier, but I was convinced I'd given it back. I had no recollection of having brought it inside, and yet Cotterell and Kits both saw me do it. The others have reported similar slip-ups, so we're all on our mettle.

Like Camp Two, the porters' highway needed clearing after the snowstorm, but it's working well again now. Despite the odd icefall, teams of Sherpas are managing lifts of stores between camps in a matter of hours, which is also allowing a brisk exchange of notes between us and poor old McLellan, down at Base.

Digging is over for the day, and it's the lull before tea. The Sherpas in the support party left a while ago for Camp One (they refuse to sleep at Camp Two), and Tenrit, Cherma, Nima, Angdawa, Dorjit and Pasang are in their tent, cooking *tsampa*. Cotterell is in ours, watching the Primuses, and Kits is over by the stores dump, sorting the last odds and ends that have been excavated from the snowdrifts down at Camp Two.

140

Garrard and I are sunning ourselves on camp stools in the lee of an enormous lump of ice, which squats by itself about ten yards in front of the tents. Nima has planted it with a stick of prayer flags, so we've named it the Sherpas' Altar.

The sun is still warm, so we're in sweaters without windproofs, but it's sinking rapidly towards the western peaks, and shadows are creeping up the slopes.

The prayer flags on the Sherpas' Altar are snapping in the wind, and the air is astonishingly clear. In this flat white glare, the guardian peaks seem so close that I feel I could leap from one to the other, like Nima's sacred snow-lions. I remember how overwhelming those peaks appeared when we were camped beside the moraine. Startling to realise that we're above them, now.

Cedric pads over and slumps at Garrard's feet. The ungrateful beast is still avoiding me, but he's been less jumpy than he was at Camp Two, and I'm taking this as a good sign. Dogs are sensitive to these things.

In front of me, and far below, stretches the vast, chaotic jumble of the Yalung Glacier. Here and there, I catch the cerulean glint of a lake. I can even make out the red dots of Base Camp. The moraines on either side of the glacier are dusted with emerald, a startling reminder that down there, it's spring. I try to picture the jungle, with those extravagant magpies — but I can't. They belong to another world.

Sitting here in the last of the sun, I'm in a state of armed peace. Camp Two is gone, and with it the dread. I'm relishing the precarious security of my little realm:

that ice cliff behind me, the Plateau in front — and beyond it, the drop to the glacier.

The pistol crack of an avalanche makes us jump. In silence, we watch the great white monster clawing its way down the Talung Saddle. By now, we've seen dozens, but you never get used to them.

Cedric has leapt to his feet, and is pressing against Garrard's leg for reassurance.

"I wonder if McLellan's looking up at us," muses Garrard, lazily scratching the dog's scruff. "I wonder if he can see us?"

"I doubt it," I say with a yawn. "I should think we'd have to go right to the edge for that."

He stretches. "Hard to imagine him down there, isn't it?"

"My God, it *can't* be!" Kits'voice rings out across camp.

"By Jove, it *is*!" cries Cotterell.

They're over by the stockpile, squatting on their haunches and staring at something lying in the snow. Cotterell is grinning, with his pipe clamped between his teeth, and Kits is flushed and excited — no, he's *ecstatic*. The Sherpas stand a little apart, their faces impassive.

"What is it?" calls Garrard.

"Come and see!"

"Seems the Sherpas overdid the excavations down at Camp Two," says Cotterell when we've joined them.

"Just *look* what they dug up!" Reverently, Kits lifts a crumpled mess of weather-stained canvas.

For once, Cedric doesn't push in to investigate. He flattens his ears and backs away. I don't blame him. The thing in Kits' hands exhales a repellent smell of mould.

Garrard is puzzled. "It's a rucksack. So what?"

Cotterell grins. "Ah, but the question is, *whose?*"

Kits thrusts the thing at me. "Take a look inside the flap, Stephen. Go on, you'll never believe it!"

But I already do. I knew the moment I saw it.

When I make no move to touch the thing, Kits flips over its front flap and shows us the underside. Sewn near the edge is a name tape: machine-embroidered, like the ones Aunt Ruth use to order by the dozen, for marking our school kit.

"Dear *God*," breathes Garrard. "It *can't* be!"

But it is. I've broken out in a cold sweat. Black spots are floating before my eyes.

Even after all these years on the mountain, the name on the tape is horribly easy to read: *ARTHUR WARD*.

CHAPTER
FOURTEEN

It's just an ordinary rucksack. Sturdily made of canvas, and weathered a leprous greenish-grey, with two outer pockets, their flaps fastened by tarnished buckles on strips of mouldy leather. It has shoulder straps of stained wool webbing, and that larger top flap, the one with the name tab, buckling over an inner drawstring, like a puckered mouth.

After three decades on the mountain, it's badly crumpled, but I'd guess that if someone smoothed it out, it would be roughly triangular, about eighteen inches along the base. I won't be volunteering. I thought once I'd put the Crag behind me, I was safe. Now this. It feels as if it's followed me up.

"I still can't believe it," Cotterell keeps saying.

By tacit consent, we've deferred all discussion of Kits' "find" until after dinner. The Sherpas are in their tent, and we've made them take Cedric. The four of us are crammed into Garrard and Kits'. I'm at one end, Kits at the other, with that thing nestled in his lap. He's staring down at it with a rapt expression, like a priest with a relic.

"Was there anything inside?" Garrard asks suddenly.

"Only this." Reverently, on his palm, Kits shows us a cheap nickel-plated match-tin with a screwtop lid. On the lid are three crudely scratched, roughly parallel lines, and two engraved initials: *AW*.

"*Where* did the Sherpas say they found it?" asks Cotterell.

"With the stores," Kits replies. "They thought it was ours, so they didn't pay much attention and can't remember where."

Garrard is frowning and pulling his beaky nose. "But how did it *get* there? I thought Ward's body fell down the crevasse."

"That was only ever surmise," says Cotterell. "No one saw it happen; the body was simply gone when Lyell and the others returned to Camp Two. It must've been blown *away* from the edge, rather than over it, then buried by the blizzard."

Garrard stops pulling his nose and gasps. "So that means — "

"*Exactly*," says Kits with startling intensity. "In *Bloody But Unbowed*, Lyell says Ward 'contrived to seize it in one hand' just before he fell. He had it with him. So there's every chance that the body's down there too! Now d'you see? We've got to go back and find it!"

I'm so horrified I can't speak.

"I say, steady on," warns Cotterell. "Think of the delay, not to mention the drain on supplies. We have to consider the implications — "

"Throw it away," I blurt out.

All three of them stare.

145

"*What?*" breathes Kits.

"Get rid of it. Chuck it down the crevasse. Dead men's things, they bring bad luck."

Garrard is aghast. Cotterell can't conceal his dismay. "But my dear fellow — you don't seriously believe — "

"Of course I don't," I lie, "but the Sherpas do, that's the point."

"Rubbish!" explodes Kits. "If they believed that, they wouldn't have touched it in the first place — "

"You said yourself, they thought it was ours." I turn to Cotterell. "You know I'm right, Major, you understand the native mind, even if Kits doesn't. We can't let this throw the porters off kilter, not now, when we're so close to making a bid for the summit. And no, Kits, we can't simply lie to them about who it belonged to; they already know, they were there when you found it!"

"We don't know that they understood," he retorts.

"Yes we do, I saw Nima's face. But don't take my word for it, ask! I think you'll find that they don't like that rucksack one little bit!"

Cotterell is stroking his beard. "You make a good point, Dr Pearce."

Garrard is nodding. "Could be wretchedly tricky if they cut up rough."

Kits is seething. He's got his bulldog look. His eyes are bulging and glassy. "Major Cotterell," he says between his teeth, "if you'll excuse us for a moment, I need a word with my brother in the other tent."

There's something farcical about "needing a word in the other tent". Simply reaching the bloody thing

146

means battling through darkness and wind-blown snow. Then once we've crawled inside, brushed ourselves off and adjusted our headlamps so that we can actually *see* each other, we have to conduct our row in strangled whispers, so that Cotterell and Garrard can't hear — or for that matter, the Sherpas.

But none of that's stopping Kits. "What's going on?" he hisses. "What's this about?"

"As I told Cotterell, this is going to play merry hell with the Sherpas — "

"The Sherpas be damned! Are you seriously suggesting that we abandon all idea of finding Ward's body? That we chuck two priceless historical artefacts — "

"Oh for Christ's sake, a match-tin and a mouldy rucksack?"

"They're part of mountaineering history!"

"Yes, and that's the crux of it, isn't it, Kits?"

"What's that supposed to mean?"

"This isn't about Ward, it's about Christopher fucking Pearce! It's about you taking your place among the great and the good of 'mountaineering history'! Conway, Lyell, Bruce, Younghusband, Mallory — and now Pearce, who won't only strike a blow for England by being the first man to conquer an eight-thousand-metre peak — thereby delivering a knockout punch to Fritz — he'll be the hero who found the missing body from the Lyell Expedition, *and* two 'priceless relics' — sorry, 'artefacts'!"

"And what the hell is wrong with that?"

I can't tell him the truth; he'll say I'm mad. "Kits, can't you *see*," I say with exaggerated patience, "we need the Sherpas if we're to have a hope of reaching the summit! Searching for a body and hanging on to that . . . thing — only lessens your chances of achieving what you want!"

His face goes stiff and his lower lip thrusts out. "You're scared. That's what this is about. You're *frightened* of a scrap of canvas!"

"Of course I'm not! I simply — "

"I saw the way you looked at it! You didn't even want to touch it!"

"Nor did the others, it's hardly inviting — "

"You never did have much guts, did you, Bodge? The fellows at school used to rag me about you; they couldn't believe we were related. And yet somehow you managed to turn it to your advantage. Stephen's the clever one, such a fine analytical mind, so bloody superior, always looking down his nose at bluff, well-meaning but just-a-bit-dim Kits."

I grin. "It's not my fault you're stupid."

"At least I'm not a coward! At least I'm not frightened of a *rucksack*! I don't think Cotterell's going to be too impressed, do you? In fact, he'll probably decide that it's high time Dr Pearce took a trip down the porters' highway, and had a rest cure with good old McLellan at Base!"

I blink. Then I force a laugh. "You really are a slimy little shit, aren't you?"

His turn to grin. "I don't know what you mean. I'm only doing what's best for the expedition."

"Which also happens to be what's best for you. Oh Kits, you're so bloody predictable! The least threat to

148

your precious self-esteem and you lash out with both podgy fists! I used to wonder if you did it on purpose, but I don't think you're bright enough. It's simply that even the lowest forms of life have some dull instinct of self-defence."

He snorts. "Why would I need to defend myself from you?"

"Because you want me out of the way. Because I'm turning out to be not *quite* such a bad climber as you'd thought. In fact, there's rather a good chance that I'll beat you to the summit — now that's what really terrifies *you*!"

Bull's-eye. His face goes puce. "*Terrified?* Terrified of *you*?"

Garrard thrusts in his head, letting in an icy blast of spin-drift. "If you two have quite finished wallowing in brotherly love, the Major wants you back in the other tent."

Cotterell hasn't found it easy to make a decision. His hairline is speckled with blood, and he doesn't meet our eyes as he waits for us to secure the tent flaps and brush ourselves off.

Kits grabs the rucksack and cradles it in his arms, as if there's a danger I might snatch it and make a mad dash for the crevasse.

"Kits, Garrard, I'm sorry," Cotterell says crisply, "but we won't be making a search for Ward's body. No argument, Kits, that's final. We simply haven't time. It's already the middle of May; if the Monsoon comes early, we'll have lost our chance at the summit. I can't allow us to run that risk."

I breathe out, and resist the temptation to shoot a triumphant glance at Kits.

"As for Ward's belongings," Cotterell goes on, "while I take your point about the Sherpas, Dr Pearce, I can't sanction discarding part of mountaineering history. We'll simply have to reassure the coolies as best we can, but these items must be preserved." Quelling my protest with a glance, he leans forwards and lowers his voice: "We'll send them down to Base in the morning, suitably concealed, so that the Sherpas don't smell a rat. Everyone agreed? Garrard? Good. Kits, what about you?"

Kits' face is thunderous. He heaves a sigh. "Agreed, sir."

"And you, Dr Pearce?"

The rucksack slumps in Kits' lap, its buckle catching the light. Winking at me.

"— Agreed," I mutter.

CHAPTER
FIFTEEN

Cotterell had returned to our tent and I was about to follow, when Kits grabbed my arm and told me to swear not to throw the rucksack down the crevasse. "Or anywhere else — in fact, swear not to touch it."

"*Swear?*" I said in disbelief. "Don't you think that's rather overdoing it?"

"I mean it, Stephen."

I glanced at Garrard, who was stowing the cooking gear and pretending not to hear. "Well if we're reverting to childhood," I said under my breath, "you swear too. No hinting to the others that there's anything wrong with my nerves!"

"Fine. You go first."

"D'you want me to prick my thumb and do it in blood, or can we agree that we're grown men?"

"Just swear."

Now I wish I hadn't. I wish I was free to chuck it down the crevasse. But Kits would have given me no peace. He never does till he gets what he wants.

He's right about one thing, though. It is only a rucksack. So why am I frightened? Why can't I bring myself to touch it? Because I meant it when I told Cotterell that dead men's things bring bad luck — but it goes further than that. In the past, you burnt the possessions of the dead, to prevent them coming after you. That's what I'm afraid of. That whatever haunts this mountain will come after its own.

I've just remembered something else, too. We can't send it off to Base tomorrow, because the Sherpas down there are having a much-needed rest, and won't be coming up to collect it. Nor can we spare a man from here to take it, as they've got to finish the ice caves. So I'm stuck with it.

Well, that settles it. Tonight I shall knock myself out with a bromide. With luck, we'll finish the caves tomorrow, so I'll be sleeping between solid walls. And after that, we'll be off for the Great Shelf, and I'll be shot of the bloody thing.

The bromide worked a treat, and after toiling all day, we finished the ice caves around teatime. Cotterell and I are in one, Garrard and Kits another, and the Sherpas are crammed into the third.

The mouth of ours is small and black and distinctly uninviting. One crawls inside and seals it with a "door" made from a canvas stuff-sack weighted with tins. The cave itself is a shadowy, downwards-sloping tunnel, with a Gothic ceiling for channelling drips. We've cut two narrow benches along the sides for sleeping. The roof above these is so low that you can't sit upright; to do that, you've got to crouch on the floor in between. At the far end, I tried to dig a storage niche, but I accidentally broke through into what appears to be another crevasse; so now it's a window, only utterly dark.

Our electric lanterns are refusing to work, so we've fallen back on the Tilley lamps. I like their glow and the smell of paraffin; and with one of them and the Primus, our cave is surprisingly warm, only a few degrees below freezing. Although it's fearfully cramped.

"Like a Pullman lower berth," mutters Cotterell, buttoning his sleeping bag. "Where's Cedric?"

"With the Sherpas." I force a laugh. "He seems to be avoiding both me *and* Kits. Or perhaps he doesn't care for that rucksack."

Cotterell makes no reply. He's overdone the digging, and has given himself a touch of heart strain. I'm treating him with Kardiazol, and I've ordered him to remain here tomorrow for a rest. Which presents me with a problem. I've been counting on climbing to the Great Shelf with Garrard and Kits, but how can I leave Cotterell?

"I think I'll stay down here and keep an eye on you," I say.

"No need for that," he gruffly replies. "I'd rather you went with the others."

"It's not only you, sir. Cherma has a touch of snow-blindness — "

"Now listen. I shall be as right as rain in a day or so, as no doubt will Cherma. If not, your excellent man Nima can help us both down to Camp Two."

I suspect Cotterell's real reason for making me go is so that Kits and I can "build bridges" during the climb; but as he remains adamant, I give in. The truth is, it suits me. The last thing I want is to stay down here. I need to put as much distance as I can between me and that rucksack.

Once the lamp is out, darkness presses on my eyeballs. I'm lying with my feet towards the door. We both are. I don't much care for this downwards slant. By twisting into contortions, I can make out a misshapen ring of dim grey moonlight around the edge of the stuff-sack. It seems a long way away.

The air is stale and chill. The deeper I breathe, the more breathless I feel. It takes a conscious effort to calm myself down. I've blocked that "window" behind me with a bundled-up shirt, but I'm sharply aware of the emptiness beyond. Putting up my hand, I touch unyielding ice, six inches above my face. It's like being trapped inside a snow globe. I wish I hadn't thought of that.

Now and then, the ice creaks and groans like a live thing. In this cramped space, every sound seems to come at me from the dark. I find myself listening for the rustle and stir of Cotterell's sleeping bag. His breathing is unpleasantly loud, and far less reassuring than it ought to be.

I tell myself that in a few hours, it'll be morning, the rucksack will be on its way down to Base, and I'll be setting off for the Great Shelf. It's a relief to discover that I do still want to climb this mountain. I'll do anything for a chance at the summit — even if it does mean "building bridges" with Kits.

Why don't I believe that any of this is going to happen? I keep assuring myself that it will, but none of

154

it feels real. At the back of my mind, there's an unshakeable conviction that something will contrive to keep me here at Camp Three.

This is hopeless. I'm sick of lying awake. Veramon, that's the ticket. Consciousness in an ice cave is overrated.

I wake to charcoal gloom and a voice whispering outside. "Doctor Sahib! Cherma's eyes very bad. Please, you come?"

Amazingly, Cotterell goes on snoring as I pull on my boots and windproofs and crawl outside. It's past four, and camp is deep in the frozen twilight before dawn. Bitterly cold. The wind is like icicles in my lungs.

The Sherpas' cave is warm with a fug of unwashed male and a spicy scent of *pan*. Poor Cherma is in agony. "My eyes melting, Doctor Sahib! They are pouring out!"

I know how that feels. When it happened to me in the Alps, I felt as if there was ground glass under my eyelids. "I promise the pills will help very soon," I tell him. "So will the drops."

Nima hands me a steaming mug of tea. "You climb today, Doctor Sahib?"

I nod. "Garrard Sahib has spotted a way up to the Great Shelf. Tenrit, Dorjit and Angdawa will come with us — but you, Pasang and poor Cherma are to stay here with Major Sahib. And Nima — "

"Yes, Doctor Sahib?"

"If Major Sahib shows the slightest change for the worse — the *slightest* — you must take him down to

Camp Two at once, whether or not he agrees. Understand?"

A shadow crosses his wrinkled goblin face. He doesn't relish the prospect of overruling Cotterell. "And the dead bag, Doctor Sahib? What is happen to it?"

The dead bag.

I clear my throat. "As soon as Lobsang and the others get here this morning, the, er, rucksack will go down to Base."

Too late, I realise that I've blown our chances of disguising the rucksack from the Sherpas. But there wasn't much hope of that anyway: they're not stupid and they always have a pretty good idea of what's in their loads.

"So there we are," I say briskly. "Soon it'll be safe with McLellan Sahib, and we can forget about it."

"Yes, Doctor Sahib." He looks puzzled, as if he's wondering whether I really believe what I've just said.

Cherma lies moaning softly, while the others quietly sip their tea. Their English isn't as good as Nima's. I've no idea how much they've understood.

"Where's Cedric?" I say suddenly.

Nima blinks. "He is not with you, Doctor Sahib? He is with us in the night, but when we are waking, he is going out."

"Stupid hound may have got lost. I'd better go and make sure he's all right."

As I set down my mug, Nima holds something out to me. "For you, Doctor Sahib. For the climb."

156

I'm astonished. It's the white ribbon-like scarf he wears around his neck, the one with the prayers. "But Nima — I can't. Your wife made it for you — "

"Is for you, Doctor Sahib," he insists with surprising firmness. "Is danger. Is good you are taking."

His expression is shy, yet tinged with pity. Does he mean something more than physical danger? Does he *know*?

To my horror, there's a lump in my throat and my eyes are stinging. I've felt so alone. To think that someone else might actually suspect what I . . . "Thanks," I croak, stuffing the grubby ribbon in my pocket and scrambling out of the cave before I disgrace myself.

Cedric isn't with Garrard and Kits, or snuffling around camp. I stomp about in the twilight, calling for him and trying to regain my composure. Grey spindrift is streaming over the ground as I trudge past the stockpile and the latrine area, towards the indigo slash of the crevasse.

I lean over the edge as far as I dare. "Cedric?"

The darkness flings back his name, but to my intense relief, I glimpse no pale, shaggy form far below.

Then I hear him, muffled whimpers *behind* me. "Oh Cedric, you daft beast!" Last night, after we finished the ice caves, the exhausted Sherpas dismantled the tents and left them at the stockpile in a tangled mound of rope and canvas — which is now faintly heaving.

Cedric's got himself thoroughly muddled, and it's quite a job unearthing him, as I have simultaneously to pin down the tents with packing crates so that they won't blow away. At last he's free, yelping with joy and slobbering all over me.

"Ha! Not avoiding me now, are you, my lad? That'll teach you to nose about in the stores! Ow!"

I'm kneeling in the snow and he's nuzzling my face when the sun's first rays touch the western peaks. My spirits lift. Over by the Sherpas' Altar, Pasang stands quietly singing a prayer, and from Garrard and Kits' cave come the usual early-morning coughs. Above me, the ice cliff is a deep shadowy blue, and above that — out of sight, yet silently calling — is the summit we mean to climb. I've been in danger of forgetting it, but it's still there in all its beauty and cruelty. No, not cruelty; it's simply a mountain: the Crystal Mountain I've longed for all my life. Nothing can alter that.

Cedric's convulsive trembling jolts me back to the present. He's panting with terror, his ears flat against his skull, his black lips peeled back. With a frantic whimper he squirms out of my grip and hurtles towards the Sherpas' ice cave.

Clouds have dimmed the sky, and suddenly I'm cold. The sun looks ill. The grey light feels troubled and wrong. The wind is still blowing, but I can no longer hear it. No hiss of spindrift, no roar over the Saddle. I can't hear Pasang singing, or Garrard and Kits coughing. The silence presses on my chest like the silence of a dream — but I'm not dreaming, I am *inside* the silence, cut off from earthly things.

My scalp is prickling, my body shrinking from what it knows is here. I can't move, can't breathe. Dread is a stone inside me, holding me frozen.

It is standing on the other side of the crevasse.

It was night when I saw it on the Crag, but now there is no merciful dark to obscure it and leave room for doubt; there is only this relentless, unnatural, diseased grey light.

I see it as clearly as I see my own mittened hands clutching my knees. I see its windproofs and balaclava and hood, all crusted with frost — so that, although it has human form, it seems made of ice. Around it, the snow is lifting and swirling in the noiseless wind, but what stands before me remains unmoved, the long tapes of its hood hanging straight. Ice rimes its snow glasses and renders it eyeless, and yet with some deep-buried part of my brain, I know that it sees. Its malevolence blasts me like the frozen breath of the crevasse: rage without end, unspeakably strong, howling eternal darkness from which there is no escape.

A voice cuts through from the other world.

With an effort, I jerk my head towards camp.

I see a corner of the Sherpas' "door" drawn aside, a slab of yellow light staining the snow. I hear Garrard calling Kits to breakfast. I hear the wind roaring over the Saddle.

When I turn back to the crevasse, the figure is gone.

But it was there. I saw it.

And worse than that, it saw me.

CHAPTER
SIXTEEN

So I was right about the rucksack. But I was wrong to feel relieved when I escaped Camp Two. I'd assumed that some kind of law confines it to the place where it was killed, like a ghost in a Victorian Christmas number, doomed to re-enact its own death. But what I saw on the other side of the crevasse isn't confined to Camp Two. And it isn't re-enacting anything.

But *why* does it haunt? That's what my mind keeps circling back to. And why is it *angry*? Did Kits stumble on the truth when he said we ought to search for the body? Is that what it wants? To be taken down the mountain and buried with its comrades on the knoll? Rest in peace, Arthur Ward?

That's not it, I'm certain. Nothing so benign. What I felt coming at me across the crevasse was no yearning for eternal rest; it was malevolence and rage, and it was directed at me.

I've just remembered another reason why ghosts walk. To warn the haunted man to prepare for death.

Is that why I'm the only one who sees it? Is it a portent of my death? I think of Cedric avoiding me, and that *gorak* perched on my tent at Base. Is that why Nima gave me his ribbon? Because I'm going to die?

"Stephen, a word." Kits is standing a few yards off with his hands on his hips, looking very solid and real.

"In a minute," I mumble.

"Now. My ice cave, chop-chop."

In a daze, I watch him trudge towards the cave mouth.

But even if I'm wildly mistaken about everything, about what I saw on the Crag and now here at the crevasse — *even if* it's all simply the result of oxygen deficiency — how does that help? The idea that altitude is giving me waking nightmares, that thin air is altering my very perceptions and deceiving my own mind into betraying me . . . I find that horrifying.

It's a kind of possession.

I'm with Kits in "his" ice cave. Garrard's here too, sheepish and embarrassed in his role as "witness".

"Witness to what?" I ask distractedly.

"To what I'm about to show you," snaps Kits. "I want you to be in no doubt that I'm keeping *my* side of the bargain."

Holding up Ward's match-tin, he stows it with ostentatious care in the rucksack, then packs the rucksack in one of the olive-green bags we use for the post.

"I've included a note to McLellan," he adds, very tight-lipped. "I've no doubt that *he* will appreciate the historical importance of what I'm entrusting to his care. There." He ties the neck of the post bag securely with a double knot. "I've told Nima to give this to

161

Lobsang as soon as the supply party gets here, with orders to take it straight down to Base. Satisfied?"

"Of course. I'd have taken your word for it, you know."

"I'd rather you saw for yourself, since it clearly matters to you so much." He speaks with studied forbearance: the long-suffering older brother, humouring the younger one's wild ideas.

Well, how's this for a wild idea, Kits? What if I sent a note of my own? *Dear McLellan, this rucksack is haunted, burn it at once.* Wouldn't that go down well?

Although on second thoughts, Kits would love that. He's made it quite clear that he thinks I'm being irrational, but he's not getting rid of me that easily. My mind is made up. I'm definitely climbing to the Great Shelf. Damned if I'll give him the satisfaction of leaving me down here, meekly caring for Cotterell, while he forges ahead for the summit.

Kits takes the lead, then Garrard, then me, then the Sherpas and finally Cedric, whom I've once again "forgotten" to send back to Base. I'm using him as an early-warning system. If anything follows, he'll be the first to know.

Luckily, we don't have to climb the ice cliff itself, as Garrard has found a way up a shadowy defile on its eastern flank. It's tricky work, hacking steps around great tumbled blocks and pinnacles (why did I *ever* long for those?). In places, the ice is so rotten that my axe sinks in with alarming ease. In others it's adamantine; I struggle to knock off shards, which fall

162

with that sinister, slithering echo. And behind everything is the dread. If it can appear by daylight . . .

An avalanche crashes past the far end of the cliff, blasting us with snow.

When it's over, Garrard gives a jittery laugh. "That was a bit close."

I don't reply. There are worse things than avalanches.

After two exhausting hours, we're above the cliff, and on to a vast whale-backed ridge, which appears to lead directly up to the Great Shelf. Kits is jubilant. "We can simply walk along it all the way!"

As usually happens, the ridge turns out to be a lot steeper than it appears. The snow is firm enough, but we're at well over twenty-three thousand feet, and the sheer effort of putting one foot in front of the other is immense. I focus my will on the rasp of my breath and my savagely aching legs. Step. Breathe. Breathe. Step. Breathe. Breathe . . .

We haven't gone far when we're spent. As we pause, chests heaving, Garrard suddenly stiffens. "What's that down there?" he gasps.

"Where?" pants Kits.

"Hundred feet down . . . On the highway" My heart turns over. Deep in the defile, a shadowy figure is following our trail.

Kits fumbles for his field glasses. "It's Pasang," he mutters.

Oh dear God, something's happened to Cotterell. I should never have left him. What was I *thinking*?

Fearing the worst, we retrace our steps down the porters' highway, towards the toiling boy.

He's nearly done up, coughing and slumped on his ice-axe. "Major Sahib worse," he wheezes. "Nima say Dr Sahib come fast!"

"But why the hell did they wait?" I explode. "I *told* Nima, any sign that he's worse and you take him straight down to Camp Two!"

The lad blinks at me through frosted eyelashes. He's scared, he doesn't understand.

"We could draw lots," suggests Kits.

"Don't be an idiot, I'm the doctor, of course I'll go!" I knew this would happen. I knew I wouldn't escape.

"Bad luck, old chap," says Kits. He's standing with his back to the edge and his snow glasses pushed up on his forehead, trying not to smirk. He knows it has to be me. He only suggested drawing lots to appear even-handed before Garrard.

I wonder what would happen if I pushed him. For an instant, I picture the shock on his face. Garrard's blank disbelief . . .

Christ knows I've not the remotest desire actually to do it, it's merely an idle thought; like the ones you get when you're in the Tube, and it flashes across your mind, *What if I jumped?* But the fact that it's occurred to me at all makes me feel awful.

I put my hand on Kits' shoulder and give it a squeeze. "You be careful up there, old man. And don't get too smug. Before you know it, I'll be joining you at Camp Four!"

I knew I'd be forced back to Camp Three, and Pasang seems to know it too. He knows I'm a marked man.

He's keeping a wary distance as we head off down the porters' highway.

So is Cedric. He's devised a novel mode of getting down the tricky bits, but it doesn't involve me. When Pasang is immediately below him, the beast half leaps, half slithers on to the lad's shoulders, then uses him as a springboard and jumps to safety. The first time he did it, he nearly knocked Pasang flying, but since then, the Sherpa digs in his ice-axe when he hears Cedric coming. I'm making them go before me, so that I can keep watch for any change in the dog's behaviour.

It's well past noon by the time Camp Three appears below us. I make out the black mouths of the ice caves in the cliff, with the stockpile and the crevasse over to the side, and in front, on the Plateau, the giant block of ice that is the Sherpas' Altar.

I can't see anyone about. With a sinking feeling, I picture Nima inside, tending a rapidly worsening Cotterell. *How* could I have left him? What if he . . .

Cedric scrambles past Pasang down the last few steps, and on to the Plateau. I watch him dart past the Sherpas' Altar and pause to sniff the wind. Then his ears go back and he's off, racing straight *past* camp. He's heading for the flags that mark the porters' highway down to Camp Two.

"Cedric!" I shout. "Here, boy! *Cedric!*"

He doesn't even glance back. In horror, I watch him dwindle to a dirty-white patch amid the glaring chaos of ice. Then he disappears.

"*Cedric!*" I'm shocked by the desolation in my voice.

165

He has wandered off before, but this feels different. This feels final. His eyes were starting from their sockets. He was terrified.

Pasang is staring at me. I mustn't lose my nerve; it'll only alarm him.

"Well," I say briskly. "I was going to send him back to Base anyway, so he's saved us the trouble!"

But inside, I'm reeling. It's terrifying how much I've come to rely on that dog. I can't believe he's really gone.

There's no one in the Sherpas' cave, or ours, or Garrard and Kits'. They're all gone. It takes a moment to dawn on me. Camp Three is deserted.

The panic in Pasang's face mirrors mine. I force a smile. "Nothing to worry about, Pasang, they'll have left us a note."

Sure enough, on Cotterell's "bunk" I find a tin of coffee pinning down a page torn from a notebook. As I skim it, my smile freezes.

"All's well," I tell Pasang, who's crouching outside the cave mouth, chewing *pan*. "Nima and Cherma have taken Major Sahib down to Camp Two. It's too late for us to follow them today. We'll stay here tonight and head after them in the morning."

The boy points to the Sherpas' cave. "I camp, Doctor Sahib?"

"You'd best bunk in here with me, it'll be warmer."

He gives an uncertain nod, and points again at the other cave. "Pasang there, yes?"

He doesn't understand; or maybe he's daunted by the idea of bunking with a sahib. "Very good," I tell him. "You settle yourself in there and make us some tea."

When he's gone, I re-read Cotterell's note.

Dear Dr Pearce, it begins in a vigorous hand that turns shaky towards the end. Earlier I was feeling grim, and Pasang panicked and sped off to fetch you. Happily, I've since improved, but your excellent man Nima has decided not to wait, and is taking me down to Camp II — against my wishes, although I understand he has orders from you & is impressively determined! Don't follow us down. I'm quite well enough to walk, & no doubt a swift descent will do the trick.

You should also know that Lobsang's supply detail (which had been and gone before all this occurred) has brought a post bag from Base. Plse take Garrard & Kits their letters; vital for morale. I repeat, don't follow me. That's a command decision. I want you where you're needed most, with G & K on the push for the summit. Sorry you've been put to this trouble. I'll write again by nxt "Sherpa post" & let you know how I go on. Yrs, Gordon Cotterell.

The silence in camp appals me. How will I get through till morning, with only Pasang?

And what's Cotterell hiding behind that military guff about "command decisions"? He's clearly desperate not to scupper the expedition, but his condition must have alarmed Nima for him to have dared to force a descent.

I'm hanged if I'll obey his "order". I need to go down there and help him as soon as I can.

It's two in the afternoon. Too late to follow them today.

Or is it? If we left now, could we make it before dark? Maybe Pasang could, but not I. After twice tackling that defile, I'm almost ill with fatigue, every muscle screaming for rest. I've no choice but to stay here. I never had a choice.

In the post bag are three bundles of letters, neatly sorted by Cotterell. Flinging mine on my bunk, I call for Pasang.

He appears at once — I suspect he's been waiting outside — and I hand him the post bag containing the letters for Garrard and Kits.

"Pack this in your *doko*. Tomorrow you'll take it up to Kits Sahib at Camp Four."

He nods. I'm unsure how much he's grasped, but I'm too drained to try again. "Very good, Pasang, you may go now."

"Yes, Doctor Sahib."

It's all I can do to pull my stuff-sack "door" across the cave mouth and weight it with tins; to light the Primus under a pan of snow, then wrap my sleeping bags around me without taking off my boots.

I must have dozed. When I wake, the light around the door is dimmer, and the Primus is hissing beneath a pan of water.

Cotterell's bunk looks disturbingly empty. It feels important that I do something about this, so on impulse, I turn it into a makeshift larder, piling it with a random assortment of provisions fetched from the back of the cave: canisters of tea and Bourn-Vita, sago, brandy balls, biscuits, the post bag . . .

The post bag? But I gave that to Pasang. He must have misunderstood me and left it here. "Pasang!" I shout.

No answer. He's probably asleep.

Muttering, I drag on my windproofs and crawl outside. It's just after three, overcast and bitingly cold.

Pasang isn't in his ice cave. He's on the porters' highway, already halfway up the defile. Bloody *fool*, he misunderstood my orders; he's heading off to join Garrard and Kits *today*.

"Pasang! Come back here!"

He's too far away to hear. Or he doesn't want to hear.

Stumbling back to the ice cave, I grab my field glasses. There he is, with his *doko* on his back, his bedroll and the post bag jutting from the top.

The *post bag*? But that's down here, I've just seen it.

Slowly, I lower the glasses. The truth crashes over me. There is a post bag in my ice cave, but it doesn't contain letters.

The post bag is waiting for me when I crawl inside. Pulling off my mittens and my gloves, I fumble with Kits' double knot and yank it open. There's a ringing in my ears. I'm spiralling into darkness. Nothing will make me put my hand into the post bag. I don't even want to look. Instead, I grasp it by the corners and upend it.

And out on to the empty bunk, with a heavy, soft thud, falls Arthur Ward's rucksack.

CHAPTER
SEVENTEEN

The rucksack slumps on the empty bunk, exhaling a musty smell of mould.

Bloody *hell*, Nima, why didn't you give it to Lobsang? Why didn't you take it yourself?

Grabbing the thing by its shoulder strap, I fling it outside, knocking over the Tilley lamp, which falls with a smash, spilling paraffin over the floor.

The stuff-sack "door" flaps in the wind, revealing a grey-green corner of rucksack. Its main flap is buckled, but I picture the drawstring mouth underneath.

Seizing my ice-axe by the head, I push the thing away. Then I crawl outside and push it further, right over to the next cave. The safety loop on my axe handle snags on one of the buckles, so that when I pull the axe back, the rucksack comes too.

"Oh no you don't," I snarl, shoving it away.

Suddenly, I see myself, a wild-eyed, shaggy-bearded tramp kneeling in the snow, fighting a rucksack. For Christ's *sake*, Stephen, get a grip on yourself! It can't hurt you. And it can't attract anything. Nothing will come after it.

Words. There's a horrible inevitability about this. Me, the rucksack, and what haunts this mountain. All here at Camp Three.

The clouds have gone, and the sky is a cold, crystalline blue. The glare is blinding. The wind is roaring over the Saddle, the prayer flags snapping on the Sherpas' Altar. By my knee, there's a scarlet spatter in the snow, where Pasang spat out a mouthful of *pan*. Pasang who is no longer here.

I am alone at twenty-three thousand feet in this wilderness of ice. I cannot *let* myself go to pieces. One small mistake, and that will be the end.

And, oh God, I've already made it. I forgot to put on my gloves. My fingers are waxy and numb.

"No no no," I mutter as I crawl back inside. I can't feel my feet, either. Fool that I was, I never took off my gaiters, they're frozen on my calves. My crampons are still on too, and caked with snow. I imagine myself with no hands or feet, nothing but black, gangrenous, frostbitten stumps.

What do I tackle first? Hands. Without them, I'm dead. Without my feet, I'm merely crippled.

"That's good," I say out loud. "That's logical. Take it step by step."

After rummaging on my bunk, I find my gloves entangled in my sleeping bag and drag them on, then tuck my hands into my armpits. The warmth hurts, and that's good too; they may only be frost-nipped.

Now for the feet. My gloved fingers are so clumsy it takes an age to unlace my frozen gaiters and get my crampons off, then begin on my boots. All the time, I'm

172

keeping a wary eye on the daylight ringing the cave mouth. Long past three. Only a couple of hours before it starts getting dark.

The Tilley lamp is past repair; I'm going to need a light, and I can't rely on my electric torch. Rummaging in the back, I'm overjoyed to find a packet of candles and a candle-lantern. My eyes sting. The old-fashioned mica casing reminds me of Aunt Ruth.

When did I last eat or drink? I find a canister of brandy balls and tip some into the hot water on the Primus. They take ages to melt, and I tire of waiting. I scoop some of the brew into my mug, and greedily drink, then sit blinking, summoning the will to act.

I'm still wearing one boot. It takes another age to remove it and peel off my socks. My feet are pallid and hard, and when I press my sole, the dent takes a while to fade.

"Fool, *fool*," I whisper. I *have* to restore circulation, but my hands hurt too much to chafe my feet, so I improvise a hot-water bottle, knotting a length of oxygen tubing at one end and filling it with the rest of the sugar water. Then I pull on three pairs of socks and wrap the tubing around my feet, tying my muffler around that to keep it on. They're already beginning to prickle, thank God.

Encouraged, I crawl to the cave mouth and scoop more snow into the pot — deliberately *not* glancing at the rucksack — then I set the pan to melt, for porridge. I'm not hungry, I'm nauseated. That's not a good sign.

I need to take stock of myself. Come on, Stephen, you're a doctor. So do some doctoring.

Apart from incipient frostbite and nausea, I have the usual high-altitude cough, but I'm not frothing or bringing up blood, so no sign of oedema. The cut on my hand isn't healing, and when I peer at my face in the saucepan lid, my warped reflection reveals a burst blood vessel in one eye, flooding the white an alarming scarlet. It doesn't hurt, though; I don't think it's serious. What troubles me more is my indecision. That's another symptom of mountain sickness. The question is, how bad?

To check my mental acuity, I name aloud the bones in the human foot. Then the hand. Good, I think I got them all. By far the best test is to walk a line heel-to-toe without falling over; but that would mean undoing the hot-water tubing around my feet, and crawling outside.

It would also give me a chance to check on the rucksack. And that's not psychosis; anyone would do the same.

The light around the cave mouth is turning grey. *What?* Ten past five *already?*

I think of shadows creeping up the mountain. I think of the long, dark night ahead.

I have to perform the heel-to-toe test. I have to be sure that I'm in my right mind. Painfully, I unwind the hot-water tubing, burying it under my sleeping bags to keep it warm, then drag on boots, mittens, balaclava, snow glasses, windproofs.

The rucksack has fallen forwards on to its face.

I say "fallen" — and yet somehow, it contrived to fall *into* the wind. And the way in which it lies suggests —

174

or would if I was mad enough to believe it — that it had been shuffling towards my cave. Or that it was pushed.

With my axe handle, I shove the thing away till it's right in front of Kits' cave, a good four feet from mine. I've lost all interest in testing my co-ordination, but I have to; that's why I came outside.

To my relief, I manage a wobbly heel-to-toe line without falling over. "Not bad, Stephen. Not bad at all!"

The sun is dipping behind the western peaks. Over my shoulder, I see Talung flush a dusky pink in the last of the light. I watch the pink cooling rapidly to mauve. A few seconds later, it fades to ash, and the brightness is gone.

Above me, clouds are clawing their way down the ice cliff. Spindrift is stinging my face and shrouding the stockpile. I can't see the crevasse beyond.

Is that what it wants? For me to end up down there in the crevasse?

When I turn to go back to the cave, the rucksack is gone. That can't be. It was right there where I left it, in front of Kits' cave.

"Where the hell are you?" I mutter, stumbling about in the snow. I have to find it; I can't bear the thought of it lying in wait.

I trip and fall. "*Fuck!*" It was here all the time, hidden under the snow. Back on my feet, I kick it again and again. "How'd you like that, eh? *Eh?*"

Why don't I throw it away? Trudge over to the crevasse and chuck it in. Or better still, march straight ahead, past the Sherpas' Altar, and fling it over the precipice. That's an awful lot nearer, and four thousand feet down: there, try coming back from *that*.

I can't do it. The precipice is twenty yards off. I dare not stray so far from my cave. If these clouds closed in and I lost my bearings, I'd be finished.

There's nothing for it. Forget about the rucksack. You'll just have to tough it out until the Sherpas get here in the morning.

I had a struggle opening the sack of sago, but I cobbled together some gritty, half-cooked porridge, and forced down a few mouthfuls. Shortly afterwards, I vomited; but most of it went on the floor, not my bunk.

I'm feeling a bit steadier. My feet and hands hurt a good deal, so with luck they'll pull through, and the cave is a balmy five degrees below. Also, I've melted more snow for tea. Well, a sort of tea-coloured brew that's cloudy with leftover sago, and fortified with apricot brandy; I found a bottle at the back of the cave, and what the hell, I need it.

Now and then, the ice around me creaks, or I hear the distant boom of an avalanche. But not even that, or the wind or the hiss of the Primus, can keep out the endless silence of the mountain.

My breath sounds harsh in this cramped little tomb. I'm trying not to think about the millions of tons of ice on top of me. All it would take is one slight readjustment, and I'd be crushed.

I find it impossible to grasp that I'm so utterly at the mercy of chance. Isn't it strange that we laugh at the Sherpas for putting their faith in amulets, when we're really exactly the same, except that with us it's a white rabbit's foot, or a crucifix? And like the Sherpas, we believe in this thing called "luck". We say: "His luck ran out", as if luck were a physical substance, rather than an illusion; it doesn't exist.

I *know* it's an illusion, but I can't bring myself to *believe* it. And I do feel better for having Nima's white ribbon in my pocket. What next? A horseshoe nailed above the cave mouth, with its ends pointing upwards, to stop the luck trickling out? I should've brought one with me from that pony I rode down in Sikkim. What was his name?

On second thoughts, I couldn't have, because he wasn't shod. But still, what *was* his name? I wish I could remember. I don't like the idea that the mountain is rubbing away my memories, like the wind erasing footprints in the snow.

When Kits and I were boys, we used to fight about who had the better memory. We fought about everything. "*Stop bickering,*" Aunt Ruth would scold, but we never did. Kits would enrage me by insisting that I had to "respect my elders" — meaning him — while I could always drive him wild simply by refusing to say goodnight after we'd climbed into bed.

The one thing we didn't fight about was that stuffed owl on the landing. By day, I was rather proud of it. After all, not every seven-year-old boy can boast a real barn owl in a glass case. But by night, I was scared rigid by its glaring eyes, its vicious talons and outstretched wings. Whenever I woke from a bad dream, and the only thing that would help was to snuggle into Nurse's bed, that owl barred my way — because in order to reach Nurse, I had to cross the shadowy landing, and creep past that dreadful winged presence. I couldn't manage it on my own, so I would shake Kits awake and beg him to take me, and he would sit up blearily: "Oh, not *again*!"

I've cut a niche in the wall above my bunk for the candle-lantern, and blocked the "window" at the back with tins and a shirt. I'm trying to summon the energy to wriggle into my sleeping bags.

The cave smells of vomit and paraffin. I ought to clean it up. And if I happen to check on the rucksack while I'm at it, so what? I need to make sure that it's where I left it, in front of Kits' cave.

Scraping up the frozen vomit with the saucepan lid, I loosen a corner of the door and fling the mess outside. To prove that I'm in control, I do this without glancing at the rucksack. Then, when *I'm* ready, I turn my head and look.

It's no longer outside Kits' cave. It's halfway towards mine, sitting upright and slightly askew, with its main flap unbuckled and flung back to reveal its puckered drawstring mouth.

"Oh no you don't," I mutter through clenched teeth. Savagely, I jab at the thing with my axe, and it flops backwards and lies there, with snow streaming over it.

Suddenly, I'm ashamed. Ye gods, Stephen, what next? Drive a stake through its heart?

I *must* have moved the rucksack without knowing it. And I must have opened it, too. There is no other explanation. The bloody thing can't have moved by itself.

I wish I hadn't thought of that. It conjures an image of it lurching blindly towards me at a slouching shuffle, its head lolling to one side.

Did I open it? Is mountain sickness making me play tricks on myself? Like that time when I brought Garrard's altimeter into my tent without realising?

There's only one way to find out. Before I turn in, I shall burn the cork from the brandy bottle and blacken my hands with soot. If, at dawn, I find the rucksack smeared with soot, I shall know that I did it in my sleep.

I'm pleased with that idea of the burnt cork. It's an empirical test that proves I'm still thinking rationally.

Before I put it into practice, though, I've some housekeeping to do. The dead skin on my fingertips is already blackening, so I pare it off with my penknife, then smear the oozing pink flesh with calamine; not forgetting that cut on my left hand. After that, I draw on my gloves, to keep the wounds clean.

By the time I've finished, my hands are throbbing viciously. But I welcome the pain. It means my flesh is still alive.

"Not doing *too* badly, Stephen old boy," I mumble. My voice is loud in the stillness. The Primus is off — although I've no memory of having done that — and the candle-lantern glimmers in its niche near my head, its flame twisting in the cold breath from the void beyond the "window".

Belatedly, I remember my improvised "hot-water bottle", and bind the tubing around my feet, securing it with my muffler, as before. The cave is a mess, so I tidy it up, laying out my bedding and neatening the supplies on the empty bunk.

Beneath the burst sack of sago, I find my bundle of letters. I stare at it, swallowing hard. The world still exists. The safe world of London and omnibuses.

My post turns out to be two fat letters from Cousin Philippa, a narrow, ominous envelope from Clare's father (that goes to the bottom of the pile), and a slender brown paper package addressed in a spidery black hand I've never seen before.

Dear God. The return address on the back is *C. F. Tennant, Juniper Cottage, near Rungneet, Darjeeling*.

The package contains several typewritten sheets, and a handwritten letter dated April 23rd: two weeks after we left Darjeeling.

I remember him hunched in his Bath chair like a battered old eagle. I remember his flinty eyes glaring up at me. We didn't exactly part on the best of terms. What does he want?

Dear Dr Pearce, he writes. *You left my house under a cloud not of your making.*

Well that's true, although surprising that he admits it.

You asked a question which brought on what my daughter calls "a turn". I've since realised that your

180

query was entirely innocent. You asked me "what sound it made", and by that, of course, you meant the *kangling,* the thigh-bone trumpet on my desk. You couldn't have known that what you said was an all too vivid reminder of something that took place on the expedition in '06 and which has haunted me ever since.

"Haunted", that's rich. I could tell him a thing or two about "haunted".

All this is a prolix way of saying that I ought not to have sent you off with a flea in your ear; nor should I have issued that rather melodramatic interdiction against attempting the south-west face. Why did I do that? I wonder. Was I trying to prevent you from repeating our mistakes? Or was I trying to goad you into making the attempt, because I regarded your expedition as my last chance? Perhaps the latter, for at the time, I cherished a hope that you might find Ward's body and lay him to rest.

Lay him to rest . . . What does he mean? Does he *know*? Did he send us here knowing what was waiting?

The ink in the next sentence is darker, as if Tennant had paused before continuing. Had he stopped to consider how much to tell me? Or did he simply need to re-fill his fountain pen?

To continue. You will recall that at one point in our talk, I asked you to hand me a box from my desk. I intended to give you what it contained, namely the memoir I am sending you now; but shortly thereafter, you posed your ill-fated question and the chance was lost.

So there we are. I don't know when, or even if the enclosed will reach you and you must make of it what you will. I wrote it earlier this year, to set the record straight about what happened on the mountain in 1906. In other words, to tell the truth about Arthur Ward.

CHAPTER
EIGHTEEN

A gust of wind sucks the door in and out, making me jump.

The truth about Arthur Ward. The words stare up at me from the page.

The lying, cowardly old bastard. Why did he wait all this time to send it? Why not when we were still in Darjeeling, or in the foothills? And why *me*? Why must *I* shoulder the burden, simply because I happened to blunder into his study?

Angrily, I toss the papers on the empty bunk. I have to get warm and ready for bed, that's the priority. I will not risk frostbite for Charles bloody Tennant.

First, I place spare candles in the lantern niche; more on the empty bunk, and my match-tin in my trouser pocket. Bottle of apricot brandy on the floor, ready for the burnt cork exercise; windproofs spread on my bunk, as insulation. Then, pulling on my extra sweater and bunching up another to form a pillow, I manoeuvre myself into my sleeping bags. The whole business is even more protracted than usual because of my gloved hands and the hot-water tubing around my feet, but at last I'm ready, lying on my stomach with the half-read letter and Charles Tennant's "memoir" before me.

I am quite startlingly reluctant to begin. Whatever these pages contain, it's explosive enough to have been kept hidden for three decades.

You will be wondering, the old man's letter goes on, why I have waited twenty-nine years to tell the truth. In part, it was cowardice. Perhaps, too, I wanted to give Edmund Lyell every chance of making his own confession. But as you are doubtless aware, he died last year in his sleep, after a serene old age and a long, happy life. I hated him to the end, for he ruined mine.

"Confession"? My stomach tightens. Can it be as bad as that?

I take no comfort from any pious hope that Lyell will receive his punishment in the next life, if such exists. There is no justice in this world, so why should we expect it in the next? But I digress. Soon I too will be dead. The enclosed is yours to do with as you think fit. There is no copy.
  Yours, Charles Tennant.

No copy? Then why entrust it to a native mail-runner? What if it had been lost en route? Or did the old man half hope that it would be? That "the truth", whatever it is, would never become known?

His narrative is entitled simply: *Memoir of Captain Charles Tennant, January 1935*. I skim the introduction, a brief but devastating character assassination of Edmund Lyell, which accords pretty well with my own

184

view of the man after re-reading *Bloody But Unbowed*, followed by Tennant's blunt statement that he wishes to *set the record straight*.

His account of the expedition completely ignores the trek to the mountain and the start of the climb, and plunges straight in at the point where, as he puts it, everything went wrong.

The early part of that day was as Lyell describes in *Bloody But Unbowed*. We had left Camp Two before dawn. Having tackled the formidable ice crag that looms over it, we were resting at the top when Ward dropped his rück-sack and, in retrieving it, fell. He came to rest, as Lyell puts it, "with a sickening crunch a hundred feet below, on the edge of the crevasse." Lyell then climbed down, found Ward dead and climbed back to us. After sending word to the baggage coolies to retrieve the body, he led us in a brief prayer and we continued the ascent.

All this happened as Lyell describes — with one significant difference, which I address in due course.

To continue. Again as Lyell describes, we had not climbed far beyond the crag when a blizzard blew up, forcing us to return to Camp Two, where we remained "snowed in" for three days. From this point on, Lyell's version of events is complete fiction.

In his book, he states that on returning to Camp Two, we learnt that the coolies had failed to retrieve Ward's body. He states that we assumed it had disappeared in the snow, or been blown into the crevasse. These are lies. Ward's body had not disappeared. As we were struggling through driving snow towards Camp Two, we were horrified to glimpse him, slumped and crusted over with ice, *on top of the crag*. I repeat, the body was atop the crag, a hundred feet *above* where he had fallen.

The conclusion was inescapable. Ward had not been killed in the fall, but merely injured. Unwittingly, we had abandoned him.

We were of course appalled. However, the body was at the far end of the crag and conditions were atrocious; it would have been madness to attempt to retrieve it. Indeed, it was all we could do to reach Camp Two ourselves.

Stratton, Freemantle and Knight took shelter in one tent, Lyell, Dr Yates and I in another. Yates and I lost no time in confronting Lyell, but he seemed as horrified as we: "When I climbed down to him, I was convinced that he was dead!"

Dr Yates took it the worst, no doubt feeling that he had derogated from his duty as a physician by not climbing down to assess Ward's condition himself. And although we never spoke of it, the fact that Ward had managed to scale the crag, despite his injuries, begged the question: how close to death had he been when Lyell had climbed down to him after his fall?

Lyell, however, remained adamant: Ward had shown no signs of life. "Besides," he added with brutal pragmatism, "he's dead now." To that there seemed no answer. I would add that we were all exhausted, the light was failing and the weather unspeakable. So we did nothing to recover the body, then or thereafter. I continued to harbour uneasy suspicions about what Lyell had found on climbing down to Ward, but I made no further enquiry. Why? Because Lyell was the expedition leader and a general. I was a captain and I was frightened.

The next three days passed in a blur, but I shall never forget the cold and the screaming wind buffeting our tents, shaking the very mountain like a thing demented. At times, there would be an eerie lull, although we could still hear the storm savaging the slopes below. At such times, I fancied that the wind called my name. This happened not once but thrice. I began to fear that I was losing my mind.

To relieve the monotony during these lulls, we six "Sahibs" often crammed together in one tent. On one such occasion, Stratton confessed to me that he had heard the wind calling *his* name. I was assailed by a dreadful thought: was it possible that it was not the wind?

Then Knight asked me if I thought ravens flew at this altitude, for he had heard strange cries. During another lull, I peered out of the tent for a breath of air and I saw something I shall never forget. I saw Ward's ice-crusted body up on the crag and I fancied that it moved its arms: awkwardly, struggling to clap its frozen fists. It only did so once or twice, and I told myself it was the wind, which still blew even in the lulls. But later, I wondered. I could not put that sight out of my mind.

That night, when we were again huddled in one tent, Freemantle quietly asked Dr Yates whether it is possible for a dead body to make involuntary movements, such as waving its arms. Yates' reply was curt: it is completely impossible. At that moment, I chanced to intercept an uneasy glance between Stratton and Knight. That was when I realised. We all knew. We knew that Ward was alive up there, and yet none of us spoke out. Perhaps we felt that it was easier to keep quiet, to let nature take its course.

Also — and I do not know if I can convey what I mean to someone who has never spent days at twenty-two thousand feet, near the limits of human endurance — there was a peculiar sense that we were "out of the world", in a place where there were no laws, no rules and no witnesses.

Heretofore, I have made no mention of Lyell himself. That is because, up to this point, he had said nothing. Nothing, that is, until Freemantle asked Yates his question about dead bodies moving, whereupon Lyell bristled and tersely forbade any more "womanish displays of nerves". I remember feeling relieved. I think we all did. The expedition leader had taken matters out of our hands.

Finally, on the third day, the blizzard ended and we emerged to a dazzling world of pristine snow. Above us on the crag, the body was gone. Whether it had been blown into the crevasse or buried beneath a drift, we were in no position to determine, as we had no strength to mount a search. Our supplies were low and we were all suffering from varying degrees of mountain sickness. We had no choice but to abandon the ascent and return to Base Camp.

None of this, of course, alters the truth. Ward had been alive up there during the blizzard. He had been alive. We had heard him crying out. We had seen him waving his arms and clapping his frozen fists. Then at some stage, perhaps as long as three days and three nights later, he had died, alone and in sight of his comrades. And we had not lifted a finger to help.

The rest of the climb is well-known and swiftly told. During our descent, we were overtaken by an avalanche. Freemantle and Knight were killed outright, Stratton and Yates dreadfully injured. For a time, I almost forgot Ward, being bent on retrieving the fallen and easing the final hours of the wounded. All this is described accurately enough in Lyell's book, albeit in nauseatingly overblown prose which accords him the lion's share of heroics. What he omits is the fact that poor Dr Yates, who was the last to succumb, regarded his own death as just punishment for having failed to go to Ward's aid. Typically, Lyell dismissed this as the ramblings of a weak mind on the verge of extinction.

The death of Dr Yates left Lyell and me the only survivors: the only ones who knew the truth about Ward. (I say nothing of the coolies, who in due course were handsomely paid off and fled to their villages, too frightened to reveal what they may or may not have known.)

On the trek back to Darjeeling, there were times when I envied my dead comrades, because for them, it was over. However, I must be clear: I did not mourn Ward. I had never cared for him. He wasn't a likeable man and he was not one of us. But he did not deserve what happened.

And always, I wondered. Had Lyell known that Ward was alive, when he climbed down to him after the fall? I wondered, but I did not ask.

On my return to England, I heard that Lyell was writing an account of the expedition, and I naïvely hoped that he would set matters straight. His book was published and he was acclaimed a hero. I was shocked. His account completely ignored the fact that Ward had survived his fall, only to perish in the blizzard. Lyell had simply omitted the entire episode.

Two years after *Bloody But Unbowed* was published, on a dismal, fog-bound Friday at the end of November, I finally mustered my courage and bearded Lyell at his Club. I asked him what he had really found when he'd climbed down to Ward on the edge of that crevasse.

His reply was measured and cool; he made no attempt to dissimulate. He had found Ward conscious and in shock, with a broken thigh. Lyell told me calmly that he had assessed the situation thus: to have rescued the injured man and helped him down the mountain would have caused such delay that, with the Monsoon imminent, we would have lost our chance at the summit. Besides, Ward would have died anyway — or so Lyell asserted. Accordingly, he said (and I found his use of that word peculiarly appalling), he abandoned the injured man and climbed back to us. Having declared that Ward was dead, he then led us in a perfunctory prayer and we continued our ascent.

190

What struck me most forcibly, as we sat in our wing chairs beside the fire, was that Lyell plainly saw nothing wrong in what he had done. "I made a command decision," he declared. "Besides, the man was dying." He seemed to have told himself this so many times that he had taught himself to believe it. Or perhaps he simply did not care. I shall never know. However, the truth remains. Ward was suffering from no more than shock and a broken leg, and he recovered sufficiently to climb the crag. He could have been saved.

At that point in our tête-à-tête, Lyell poked the fire and rang for whisky and soda. It was bizarre. We might have been speaking of billiards, not the protracted and agonising death of a companion.

When we were settled with our drinks and once again alone, I brought the talk round to those three days when Ward had been on the crag and we were down in Camp Two, sheltering from the blizzard. Finally, I mustered the courage to admit that we had all known that Ward remained alive. At this, Lyell became impatient. "Well, and what of it? The man was dying! And I didn't see you climbing up there to bring him down, or Knight, or Freemantle, or Stratton, or Yates!"

"Be that as it may," I replied, "will you make a clean breast of things now?"

At that, he opened his eyes wide and gave me a condescending smile. "My dear fellow, what on earth would be the point?"

"Then I will," I retorted.

Still smiling, he regarded me askance. "They won't believe you, you know. A man who has been in and out of rest homes and consulted alienists for his nerves? They will say that you're deranged — and jealous of my success. They will say that if there had been a shred of truth to your story, you wouldn't have waited all this time to tell it."

He was right. Or so I chose to believe at the time, because it suited me to keep quiet. Because I am a coward.

So there we have it. I have kept my silence for twenty-nine years. During that time, I have often thought of speaking out — indeed, it feels as if I have thought of little else. That has been my punishment.

As for Edmund Lyell, in the course of his long, happy life, I do not believe that he ever experienced a moment's disquiet.

CHAPTER
NINETEEN

Slowly, I re-fold Tennant's memoir, and replace it with his letter in the envelope. I put the envelope in my kitbag on the empty bunk. I find my match-tin and my cigarettes, and after a few attempts, I light one and suck on it hard.

People used to have ways of protecting themselves from the dead. "It's not out of respect that folk wear black," Nurse used to say. "Oh no, it's to fool the dead, so they can't come after you. And don't you speak ill of 'em, neither. And never keep nothing that was theirs, that's sure to draw them." Anything to avoid attracting the angry dead.

And it is angry, no doubt of that. And now I know why.

Three days in a blizzard with a broken femur. Knowing you've been abandoned, within sight of camp. And I'm fairly sure that he did survive for the full three days, because of those three jagged lines scratched on his match-tin.

For twenty-nine years, Tennant has lived with the guilt. Hunched in his study with its view of the mountain, and that thigh-bone trumpet on his desk, a reminder hidden in plain sight. "Every night, do you

193

understand, I see them . . . Yes, I shall always see them." But he'd been talking about Ward.

No wonder he collapsed when I asked him what it sounded like. I meant the trumpet, but he was thinking of something else; and he knows what it sounds like because he heard it: the cries, the muffled thud of frozen fists.

Poor cowardly, self-hating, self-deluding Tennant. Even now, when he purports to "set the record straight", he can't quite bring himself to face the whole truth. He has to depict Lyell as the chief offender — when in fact they were all equally guilty. They knew Ward was alive. Why didn't they climb up to the "body" during one of those lulls? Why does Tennant keep referring to it as "it"?

He gives himself away when he says that Ward "was not one of us". That's the real reason they didn't rescue him. It wasn't fatigue or mountain sickness, or "atrocious conditions", but the oldest reason of all: Ward wasn't one of them.

If he *had* been — if it had been Freemantle or Knight dying on the Crag, or Stratton or Yates or Tennant, or Lyell himself — they would have risked life and limb to save him; as indeed they did after the avalanche.

I've just realised something else. I've been asking myself *why* it haunts. I've assumed that it must have a reason — to right some wrong, or be avenged — and that once I know why, I can fix it, and this will be over.

But how can you right this wrong? Ward died a lonely, agonising death that could have been prevented.

194

Nothing can atone for that. Nothing can right that wrong.

If McLellan were here now, he would no doubt pray for Ward's repose. But I'm as certain as I can be that what haunts this mountain can't be "laid to rest", and it can't be appeased. It exists to terrify and appal. It doesn't matter that I'm innocent and I've done it no harm. I'm alive. That's enough.

And perhaps this won't even be over when I'm dead, no not even then, when what remains of me lingers on in this dreadful place, conscious and without hope of release . . .

The candle-lantern flickers and goes out.

I cower on my stomach, fighting panic. The darkness is a wall, pressing on my face.

The lantern went out because I forgot to replace the candle, *that is all*. My headlamp and my electric torch are readily to hand on the empty bunk.

Except that they're not, because I forgot to put them there, I forgot all about them. Are they in my kitbag? My rucksack? They might as well be at the bottom of the crevasse. Nothing will make me plunge my hands into canvas in the dark.

At my feet, I make out a charcoal glimmer around the cave mouth. That can't still be twilight, can it? Moonlight? Snow glow? I've no idea what time it is, and my watch isn't on my wrist, although I don't remember taking it off.

Groping for the lantern niche, I find a spare candle. I extract my match-tin from my pocket and unscrew the lid . . . I drop the bloody thing, scattering matches.

As I'm scrabbling for them, the glimmer at the cave mouth briefly cuts off.

I freeze like a trapped animal. Something has just passed my door.

The wind has died. The silence is appalling. My mind scurries in ancient, deep-buried channels of thought. Nothing exists but the menace outside.

The "door" slaps, jokingly loud. The wind moans. It's gone.

I force myself to grope in the dark for a match. At last I find one, and strike a light. Shadows leap as the blessed flame flares to life.

"There, now," I whisper, setting the lantern in its niche. "There."

At the back of the cave, my shirt has come loose from the "window", releasing a chill breath from the nothingness beyond. Hastily, I stuff it back in.

The "window" is gone. I'm lying half over the crevasse, with the Crag looming over me. There's something dreadfully wrong with my leg. An extra bend at mid-thigh, like a broken doll.

Far above, I make out the others, peering over the edge of the Crag. Now a man on a rope is climbing down to me. *Thank God.* They'll find a way to rescue me. I'm going to be all right.

"Thank God," I whisper as he bends over me.

Through his snow glasses, his eyes meet mine. No emotion. I might as well be a lump of ice.

Raising his head, he shouts to the others: "He's dead! I'm coming up!"

196

What? What does he mean? He can't — he can't be *leaving* me? He knows I'm alive, he heard me speak. His eyes met mine.

He's already climbing, his boots sending shards of ice spattering on to my face. And on top of the Crag, not one of the others remonstrates with him, or shouts, "Are you sure he's dead?"

I try to cry out — to scream and howl — but I only manage a groan. *You bastards. Leaving me alone in the cold and the dark. Leaving me to die . . .*

With a cry, I jerk awake. My shirt sleeve hangs limply from the "window". The breath of the void chills my face.

I try not to think of it, but my thoughts keep circling back. I feel dizzy and sick. I can't let myself go to sleep again. I don't dare.

Christ, it's quiet in here. How I miss Nima's flute and Pasang's tuneless singing; Cedric snuffling about, Kits whistling between his teeth . . .

They're all gone. Even that *gorak* has abandoned me. It's as if they planned it.

From my pocket, I pull Nima's ribbon. I remember his expression when he gave it to me: the pity in his brown eyes.

Or was it apology? Did he know I was going to be left on my own?

And why didn't he give Lobsang the rucksack to take down to Base? Did Lobsang refuse? Or was Nima so worried about Cotterell that he forgot? Or did he leave it here on purpose?

If they did abandon me deliberately, I think I can guess why. Being haunted isn't only a portent of your own death. The harm spreads further, like a stain. A haunted man is a danger to others. Is that why Nima and Pasang left? And Cedric?

Did they all know?

Smearing on the burnt cork has taken ages, but it's worth it to prove my rationality. My gloved hands are now black with soot. I found my wrist watch, too, under the sack of sago. Heaven knows how it got there.

Every breath is a struggle in this thin, dead air. I can feel every thud of my labouring heart. It's an effort to keep my eyes open, but I refuse to give in. I lie watching the flame twisting in its little mica house. I clutch my talismans to my chest: match-tin, wrist watch, Nima's ribbon.

Time is elastic. The minutes stretch like hours, the hours snap by in moments. I find the little luminous dials on my watch reassuring. They show me time neatly cut into even pieces.

The ceiling of my cave isn't as close to my face as I'd thought. In fact, it's not a ceiling, I'm lying on top of the Crag, staring up at a black sky thick with fast-falling snow.

I'm still clutching Nima's ribbon, but my wrist watch is gone — and where's the match-tin?

It's here beside me. I must not let go of it again.

A few yards off, a man in old-fashioned climbing gear sits slumped on his side. His balaclava and windproofs are crusted with ice. Something is wrong with his leg.

I am that man. I am clutching the match-tin in rigid fingers. I must not let go.

My eyelids are frozen open, I can't even blink. Snow scours my eyeballs like ground glass, but I can't brush it away. A jagged point of bone juts through the leg of my climbing suit. I need to push it back in, but I can't move. I'm imprisoned in an icy carapace of frozen windproofs.

The snow rips apart, and down below, I make out a camp with tents. I see men moving in the yellow beams of lanterns. Hope glimmers. I shout for help. My lips are too stiff to shape the words, and the wind snatches away my wheezy cries.

Above me, the stars turn. The moon and the sun wheel across the sky — and always the wind and the snow attack. With an awkward, agonising jolt that grinds my shattered bone into my flesh, I bring the match-tin to my mouth, and drag it under my teeth, to mark the day. Pain stabs my brain. A tooth has snapped off. Blood pours from my mouth, freezing in a heartbeat.

Down in camp, a man's head pokes out of one of the tents. It's Tennant. I recognise his helmet.

Now he's trudging towards the foot of the Crag. He's seen me!

With his mitten, he wipes his snow glasses. He raises his field glasses. I try to shout. I thud my frozen fists together. *Help me!*

He has seen me. He is staring straight at me. His face doesn't move and he makes no sound. Slowly, he lowers the field glasses. He turns and trudges back to the tent and disappears inside.

He doesn't come again. He only came to look. I am not a man, I am a lump of meat. He has left me alone in the cold and the howling darkness. Forever alone. Blood seeping from my shattered thigh, snow like ground glass filling my nose and mouth, scouring my eyeballs —

I wake with a gasp.

The darkness is absolute. The candle is dead. The wind is sucking the door in and out.

I lie panting and shuddering, willing the nightmare to fade. I was trapped in that carapace of ice, but appallingly alive, appallingly aware . . .

Gradually, the nightmare recedes, and my breath slows. The sweater that forms my pillow is scratchy beneath my cheek. Beyond my feet, I make out a faint grey glimmer around the mouth of the cave. I lie watching the stuff-sack sucking silently in and out. With a sigh, I turn over and bury my face in my pillow . . .

— it isn't my sweater. My face presses into something crumpled and cold. I inhale the dank smell of mouldy canvas. With a scream I recoil, falling back against the empty bunk. The rucksack is in here with me; it's inside my sleeping bag.

And the other bunk isn't empty. Behind me I hear the stiff rustle of frozen windproofs. In the grey gloom, the darkness moves, and I make out a dim, humped form.

Terror washes my mind white: for a heartbeat, I can't see, can't hear. I scramble for the door, but the sleeping

200

bag is twisted round my legs, and my feet are tangled in the muffler and the hot-water tubing. The thing on the bunk heaves and comes after me. I squirm on my belly towards the cave mouth, kicking free of the bindings and the sleeping bag. One foot sinks into something that rustles and wraps around my ankle. Mewing, I thrash, clawing ice, hauling myself forwards — I burst out of the cave.

The wind is a knife in my lungs as I lurch to my feet and stagger into the grey twilight. Over my shoulder, the cave mouth is utterly black, but at any moment, a dim hunched form will emerge and come after me.

Now I'm at the edge of the crevasse. How did I get here?

I'm swaying and clutching the rucksack in one hand. "No more," I gasp. "*No more!*"

Yelling, I fling the rucksack into the crevasse.

"There now," I pant. "Finished. No more."

Behind me, ice clatters glassily down the cliff.

I'm standing by the Sherpas' Altar, although I've no memory of having staggered back from the crevasse. I'm not wearing my boots or my windproofs, I'm in gloves without mittens, and stockinged feet; but I'm still clutching my ribbon and my wrist watch.

It's twenty to five. Thank God. Not long till dawn.

Somewhere above me, a voice shouts: "*Below!*"

My heart stops. I thought it was over. I thought when I chucked the rucksack into the crevasse, that would be the end.

"*Below!*" The voice echoes from peak to peak.

A snowball thuds into my chest — and there is Kits at the foot of the defile. "Hulloa, Bodge! Coming to meet us?" And behind him are Garrard and Tenrit, Angdawa, Dorjit and Pasang, grinning as they make their way towards me down the porters' highway.

CHAPTER
TWENTY

"Good *Lord*, Bodge, where are your boots?"

Kits is no longer grinning, and neither is Garrard. The Sherpas are staring at me open-mouthed.

"Th-thank God you're here!" I stammer as I stumble towards them. "If we leave now, we can make it back to Base — "

"What are you talking about?" cries Kits.

"I'll take him inside," mutters Garrard. "Get him warmed up."

"*Listen* to me — "

"For Christ's *sake*, Bodge, what is this nonsense? It'll be dark in an hour!"

"What d'you mean?" I shout. "It's five in the morning, it's just getting light!"

There's silence.

"Stephen," says Kits in an altered voice. "It's five in the afternoon. Now shut up and come inside."

I don't understand how it happened. While I was in that cave, I lost a whole day. And now the night has been and gone, and I'm still here at Camp Three.

I flatly refused to re-enter my own ice cave, so Garrard took me to his. He stayed with me while

Pasang fetched my things, then he warmed me up and saw to my feet.

Some time later, a newly recovered Cherma arrived from Camp Two with a note from Cotterell, which Garrard read aloud: "*Improving by leaps and bounds, fighting fit in a day or so . . .*" I'd forgotten about Cotterell. So much for my duty as a physician. Although I didn't even feel guilty. I was too dazed.

At dinner, I devoured four mugs of tea, a packet of Ginger Snaps, and a saucepanful of tapioca smothered in Golden Syrup. Normality returned — except that it didn't, not for me. I told myself I was safe with all these people; that with the rucksack gone, there was nothing to fear. The rucksack was what drew it, so now it couldn't come after me. But I didn't believe it. I felt cut off from the others. I felt like the ghost at the feast. Ha ha ha.

Garrard was unusually subdued, but Kits was in high spirits, going on about a possible route to the summit, and how splendid it had felt to be the first man ever to set foot on the Great Shelf; this with a pitying glance at me, the younger brother who'd lost his nerve and worked himself into a funk.

If only Kits knew how profoundly I no longer care about the summit. While he was talking, I kept thinking: he doesn't know. None of them knows.

Then I became aware that he and Garrard were hatching plans to climb back to Camp Four in the morning. "You can't do that," I said in a low voice.

They exchanged glances.

"I can't explain now," I said, "and you wouldn't believe me if I did, but there's something terribly wrong with this place. We have to get the hell off this mountain as fast as we can, or something dreadful will happen."

Garrard sat pulling his nose and avoiding my eyes. Kits blew out a long breath. "Listen, old chap. It was rotten luck that you were here on your own, and you had a few bad dreams, but it's *over*."

"I don't care what you think, as long as we leave."

His eyes turned hard. "Do you have any idea of the state you were in?"

"That doesn't — "

"Filthy with *soot*? Waving your arms like a madman? No boots, no windproofs — "

"I'm not mad," I said between my teeth.

"I didn't say you were. But I am *not* about to scupper this entire expedition because you say so. According to the Sherpas, we've a few days' good weather *at best*. That's why we came down. I need every available man carrying supplies to Camp Four, so that we can make the push for the summit — "

"To *hell* with the summit!" I exploded.

Kits continued as if I hadn't spoken. " — and with Cotterell still *hors de combat*, I believe I have seniority. We leave at four thirty. As for you, Stephen, you do what you bloody well like."

There was no arguing with him, and soon afterwards, we turned in, Kits pigging it with Pasang in my ice cave, and me with Garrard in his. Just before he snuffed out the candle-lantern, Garrard asked what I meant by "wrong". But I couldn't talk about it in the dark, so I brushed him off. And I'd already taken a Veramon, to knock myself out.

Next thing I knew, it was four fifteen and we were fastening our crampons. The ice cave was loud with breath and the rustle of windproofs. I got out of there as fast as I could.

Now it's the grey twilight before dawn. And this time it really is dawn: bitterly cold, but not much wind. The sky is heavy with snow, and the clouds are tinged with green. The Sherpas stand waiting in clouds of frosty breath.

As we head across the Plateau, it begins to snow, a light, insidious pattering on my hood. I can just make out the red flags of the porters' highway, snaking up the defile to the right of the ice cliff.

Our headlamps are pinpricks of yellow, swallowed by the gloom. Kits is in the lead. I'm next, with Garrard behind me, followed by the Sherpas. We're unroped, and it occurs to me to wonder if this is wise; but the ice steps don't become steep until we reach the whale-back ridge.

And I have to climb with them to Camp Four because I'm not brave enough to descend to Base on my own. Although in fact I doubt whether I'll be allowed to escape from Camp Three. I tried before, and things conspired to bring me back. Why should it be different now?

We pass the Sherpas' Altar, and I stop to knock the packed snow from under my crampons with the butt of my axe. It's not easy; my hands are hurting again. I can't even feel my feet. They're probably frostbitten. I no longer care.

I hear the crunch of Garrard coming up behind me. His beard is white with frost. With his fist, he rubs his snow glasses clear. "What did you mean last night," he pants, "when you said something's wrong?"

"Not now, Beak."

"D'you think — there's something here? Something bad?"

Something bad . . . A jittery laugh bubbles up in my throat. Then, through his snow glasses, I see the terror in his eyes. I feel as if I'm falling. "You've seen it too."

He glances over his shoulder to check that the Sherpas are out of earshot. "Don't tell Kits, he'll think I'm — "

"When? What did you see?"

"Yesterday. On the ridge, just before we reached the defile." He licks his lips. "It was following. Broad daylight . . . Unspeakable."

"Come on, you lot!" calls Kits, up ahead.

"*Don't* tell him," Garrard mutters fiercely.

I stare at the Sherpas' Altar, my thoughts in a whirl. A few days ago, we sat here chatting in the sun, on the afternoon they found the rucksack. Did I bring it inside the ice cave without knowing? I must have. And it must have been smeared with soot when I threw it down the crevasse. But I can't remember.

Besides, what does that matter now? Garrard has seen what I've seen. It isn't only me.

The steps of the porters' highway are glassy and uneven. We haven't climbed far up the defile when suddenly the snow is coming down much thicker and faster. Within moments, it's a white-out, cutting us off from each other. I can hardly see Kits' headlamp. I'm shut in with the snow, my breath loud in my ears, my windproofs caked and stiff.

We struggle on, but it's impossible. Garrard's voice drifts up from below: "This is hopeless, we have to turn back!"

Above me, Kits is almost out of sight, still doggedly climbing.

"Kits!" I yell. "We have to turn back!"

His headlamp blinks out. Then I hear him. "Agreed! Everyone back to camp!"

"Back to camp!" I shout down to Garrard and the Sherpas.

So ends my second attempt at escaping Camp Three.

Climbing down the defile is harder, as I can't see the steps. I jump the last four feet on to the Plateau. Snow up to my knees, whiteness whirling around me. For a moment, I don't know where I am.

I manage a few steps, and the Sherpas' Altar looms into sight. I slump against it. I make out Garrard struggling towards the caves. Somewhere above, I hear Kits: "Stephen! Where are you?"

"At the Sherpas' Altar!" I shout back. "I'll wait here till you're safely down!"

"Right-ho!"

He doesn't appear, and I'm beginning to worry when I glimpse him, feeling his way with his axe down the last of the steps.

208

Garrard has tired of waiting by the caves and is trudging back towards us with his head down.

"I'm waiting for Kits," I pant as he approaches. "You stay here at the Altar! I'll go and meet him — "

It isn't Garrard.

Silence like a white wall, shutting me in. No crunch of footsteps, no rustle of frozen windproofs. It is hooded and faceless and crusted with ice. Its rage blasts me to my knees.

With the slowness of a dream, I flounder to escape. Kits is calling my name. I open my mouth, but I can't make a sound. It's nearly upon me. I slip and fall. Can't get up. The snow has balled beneath my crampons.

It is so close I could reach out and touch it. If it comes another step nearer, my heart will burst.

With a convulsive heave, I fling myself sideways. Over my shoulder, through swift-falling snow, I see it pass. I see the rucksack on its back.

"Stephen, where are you!" yells Garrard — the real Garrard, labouring towards me.

Again Kits shouts, "All right, Stephen, I can see you now!"

But I can't see him. Where *is* he?

Then the billowing whiteness rips apart — and there he is. He has passed the Sherpas' Altar without seeing it, and instead of making for the caves, he's heading in the other direction, trudging towards the ice-rimed figure that stands waiting. I open my mouth to scream a warning, but what comes out is a nightmare wheeze. It's Garrard who screams, a dreadful animal shriek: "*Kits turn back, you're going the wrong way! You're too near the edge!*" But Kits doesn't hear, and as he reaches the thing he's mistaken for me, there's a deafening boom and a vast slab of ice breaks beneath him —

— and he isn't there any more.

Kits is gone.

CHAPTER
TWENTY-ONE

People don't cry out when they fall. Kits didn't. He made no sound at all.

I stood with the snow pattering on my hood, random thoughts tumbling through my mind. Who's going to tell his wife? Thank God Aunt Ruth will never know. How can he be gone?

Then Garrard was screaming and staggering straight for the edge. "Oh God Kits no no no!" I was pulling him down and he was lashing out at me, and the Sherpas were coming and we were dragging him back to the caves. We had to tie him up, and I gave him a sedative and held him while he cried great wrenching sobs. I didn't cry, not then. I couldn't believe that Kits was gone.

We found out later that McLellan had watched the whole thing through his field glasses from Base. He'd seen what we couldn't: that the edge of the Plateau was one vast overhanging cornice, which had broken off and taken Kits with it.

McLellan didn't want to tell me the details of what he'd seen, but I forced him to.

"It happened slowly," he said that first night at Base, as we worked our way through two bottles of Scotch.

"The cornice just seemed to peel off, not jerky or fast, and he simply dropped. And God forgive me, I couldn't look away. Halfway down, he — he struck a spur. He went wheeling out into the air, then down again hard, a fast jolting slide. I lost him . . . Then I saw something dark lower down, sliding slower and slower till it — he — finally stopped."

I asked what he meant by "something dark", but he would never say.

I also asked what he'd seen immediately *before* Kits fell. He didn't mention seeing anyone else on the edge, so I'm quite certain that he saw only Kits. I don't know about Garrard. All he's ever told me is that he saw me on my knees, frozen with horror and staring at Kits, just before the ice broke.

I don't remember much about those first days at Base, apart from Cedric's howls. He'd found his way back, and had been keeping McLellan company; but after the accident, the Scotsman tied him up to stop him bothering us. He howled for hours. Once, Cotterell brought him to see me, but he cringed and whimpered in terror, so Cotterell took him away. We never tried it again. I hated to see the poor beast so terrified. He's better off with McLellan.

I'm told that I was remarkably composed during that time, and that I kept saying, "We can't leave Kits, we have to bring him back." So they did. McLellan had seen where he fell, and without telling me, he, Cotterell and Nima went to find him. They brought him back in his sleeping bag. Cotterell was grimly silent; I daresay

212

he was used to such things from the trenches. Nima was shaking. McLellan's freckled face was grey.

They tried to keep the truth from me, but I found out. Kits wasn't whole. How could he be, after striking that spur, then that "fast jolting slide" over the granite and the rough Himalayan ice?

The others had collected what they could find, but it wasn't enough to fill a coffin. Only a small packing crate. Or maybe a rucksack.

When we were boys, Aunt Ruth's mountaineering stories always ended at the mountain. She never mentioned the fact that you've got to get back.

I'm told that I "kept myself together splendidly" during the trek, but the truth is, I didn't feel a thing. I was an automaton: looking after Garrard, helping Cotterell and McLellan prepare reports for the Himalayan Club in Darjeeling and the Alpine Club in London. Although I do remember coming off the glacier near Yates' cairn, and realising in disbelief that we were back in the world and it was spring, a skylark trilling overhead, green grass and blue Himalayan poppies.

The next morning, I climbed the moraine and said goodbye to the mountain. I thought: that lump of rock and ice will be there when the human race has broken and receded like a wave. It will never know what dreams and fears it has inspired, or what fierce desire. It will never know what haunts it.

Then a cold grey curtain of rain came down and hid everything from view. That was the start of the Monsoon.

I "kept myself together" till Darjeeling, where I rather spectacularly fell apart. I remember sitting with Nima and Cotterell in a horse-tonga outside Tennant's bungalow. Then I was leaning over the old man in his Bath chair, screaming: "Did you *know*? Did you *know*?"

After that, I recall being dragged back to the tonga, and torrential rain and watery greyness, everything muffled — and crying in Nima's arms as I'd never cried before.

Two days later, Tennant died of a heart attack. *Did* he know? Were he and Lyell haunted during their last days on the mountain?

Re-reading what they wrote, I've found the odd phrase which might suggest that they were. That bit at the beginning of Tennant's memoir about the mountain killing five, but they'd only laid to rest four. And somewhere in *Bloody But Unbowed*, Lyell mentions *something wrong about the air*, and *an uncanny silence* . . . Although I may be inferring too much. And Tennant did say that Lyell never experienced a moment's disquiet.

Besides, even if they did know — even if Tennant had warned me that first night, before we set off — I wouldn't have listened.

Cotterell was marvellous on the voyage home. He handled Garrard with touching gentleness, and read aloud to me when I didn't dare sleep: *The Vicar of Wakefield*, and three of the Barchester novels.

214

I missed Nima dreadfully. He'd come with us to Bombay, and stayed with me while they amputated my toes. To my shame, the only way I could show my gratitude was by giving him money; but he was delighted. He said that when he returned to his village, he would buy many yaks. When I asked him to write to me, he smiled and said gently that he'd never learnt how. So it really was goodbye.

For a long time, I blamed myself for Kits' death, because I didn't shout a warning. I still wonder. Was I *really* incapable of crying out? Couldn't I have tried harder? I'll never know. What I cling to is the fact that I never told him I'd chucked the rucksack, or about Tennant's memoir. So he died believing that Lyell and his companions were heroes. At least I got that right.

Kits' widow blamed me too, on the one occasion I visited her. She couldn't understand why I didn't warn him, and I couldn't tell her. Garrard, who was with me, assured her that it wouldn't have done any good, that Kits was already right on the edge; but she didn't believe him. As we were leaving, she looked up into my face and said stonily, "You always wanted to beat him. Well, now you have."

She can't truly believe that, not in her heart. And in what way have I won? Thank Christ I didn't inherit a penny; it's all gone to the boys.

For weeks after Kits' death, I hoped he would visit me in a dream and tell me he's all right; but he never has. And surely that's a good sign? It means that for him, death was the end? God, I hope so. Once, in Bombay, Nima tried to explain to me why he doesn't fear dying: because it's merely a transition to another existence. I couldn't find the words to convey to him that after what happened on the mountain, another existence is what I dread above all else.

I've spoken to several people who've survived falls while climbing, and they tell me that one feels no fear and no pain, there isn't time. I hope — although hope is too weak a word for the intensity with which I want this to be true — that it was like that for Kits. And I hope that he never knew what was waiting for him on the edge: that all he saw was rushing whiteness and after that nothing, blackness, gone. No lingering consciousness in that wilderness of ice, with the thing that walks.

It's been three years, and I still correspond with McLellan. He's remained in India, even though he knows that it won't be long before the whole bloody Raj goes to smash. I've told him that on his next home leave, he must come to me, but so far he hasn't been over. I suspect that he doesn't care to leave Cedric — although he'd never admit it.

A publisher offered me a great deal of money to write an account of "the tragedy", and when I refused, Garrard wrote one instead, as a memorial to Kits. He made no mention of what he'd seen on the mountain, or of the state I was in at Camp Three, and we've never spoken about it. His book has become a "best-seller". Well it would, because somebody died. It has allowed Garrard to buy a house in Marrakesh, and I've heard nothing from him since.

Publishers keep urging me to write "my side of the story" — but who would believe that? And to write it would be to relive it, which is something I can't do.

Besides, I've been thinking about the chain of events that led me and Kits to Kangchenjunga. It began in the nursery with the Crystal Mountain; then *Bloody But Unbowed* when we were boys. That's the real reason I shall never write anything. I couldn't bear to think that any book of mine might inspire someone else to trek out there, and go through what I did.

Of course, my dream of practising medicine in Sikkim never happened. I cling to London's narrow, crowded streets. Clare's father dropped his legal action — he said I'd been punished enough — so I was able to buy a small general practice in South Kensington. I'm doing rather well. I think people come to me because they're curious, or they feel sorry for me.

Cotterell was quietly devastated by Kits' death. He's aged a good deal, and I often visit him at his little estate in Sussex. I can't take Kits' place in his affections and I don't try, but we like each other. He enjoys talking about Kits, and as he lives quite close to where our family used to have their seat, we visit the parish churchyard, and Kits' grave.

Bringing him back was something else I did right. When we were still on the glacier, I kept his remains on ice. When we reached the moraine, I packed him in salt. Nima helped me; another astonishing act of kindness that I can never repay.

Of course, I don't really believe that any trace of who Kits was lingered on in that poor, mangled flesh, but I couldn't leave him behind. I couldn't bury him on the knoll, or with Yates by the moraine. So I brought him home. The "remains", I mean. And I refuse, I absolutely refuse, to believe that any part of him is still on the mountain with that thing.

Grief is a lumpy, uneven affair. Sometimes I'm *angry* with Kits: for being so bloody thoughtless and unimaginative and *irritating*. Fucking hell, Kits, you didn't have to die. Enough! *Pax.*

And how he would hoot with laughter if he knew about the salt. "Good Christ, Bodge, you've gone and *pickled* me!"

That's the worst of it, not being able to laugh together. Except it isn't the worst, I keep discovering new "worsts". It's as if I'm trying to touch bottom, but I haven't, not yet.

Maybe it's been even worse for Garrard. Once in Bombay when we were alone, he said, "He was my best friend. My best and only friend."

"I know," I replied.

He glared at me with sudden hatred. "You didn't even like him, did you?"

I hesitated. "No. Not much. He didn't like me, either. We were too different."

"So why pretend to grieve?"

"I'm not pretending."

Garrard was puzzled, but I couldn't explain. He's an only child; how could he understand? Kits and I *didn't* like each other, but we were brothers. We were caught in a messy tangle of love and hate, cruelty and guilt, illumined by the occasional flash of sympathy — like

218

that time at Camp Three when we were digging the ice caves, and everything felt right. Now that messy tangle has been chopped in half, and I'm alone. There's no one who remembers Aunt Ruth reading aloud from *Scrambles in the Alps*; or the stuffed owl on the landing. There's no one to call me Bodge.

That owl. When we were boys, Kits was a great one for practical "jokes" of varying degrees of nastiness. But no matter how often I woke him after a nightmare and begged him to take me across the landing, past that wretched owl, he never made a joke of it. And he never once refused.

I felt cold for months after we returned to England, although it was a beautiful summer. Even today, on a sunny May afternoon, with sparrows chirping in the elm tree and people in their light summer clothes strolling along the pavement beneath my window, I'm huddled by the fire with a rug over my knees. The mountain is still with me. I carry it inside. I always will.

Yesterday, I was in Hatchards, and I saw a photograph of it, the usual view from Darjeeling. Everything flooded back. The cold, the silence. The dread. It was so overwhelming that I staggered outside and vomited in the gutter. People thought I was drunk.

I experienced the same thing last year, when I re-read Tennant's memoir one final time before I gave it to the Alpine Club. In answer to my most recent enquiry, they told me they've not yet decided whether to make it public. I don't care what they do. I've no illusions that exposing the truth will lay the ghost. Nothing will. It's still there. I saw it this morning.

The dream was the worst it's ever been. It always comes before dawn, in the dim grey light. I wake, and I'm back there in the snow, just before Kits falls. Only this time, I *do* shout a warning, and he turns and starts trudging towards me, *away* from the edge. Then I become aware that that thing isn't with him, it's with *me*. The silence is shutting me in, and it's coming closer, I can't bear it, my heart is going to burst —

That's when I always wake up, clutching Nima's ribbon. But this morning when I woke, I realised with a sickening plunge that everything that's happened since Kits died — the trek back, the voyage home, London, everything — it's all been a dream. I never left the mountain. *I* was the one who fell. I'm there now, trapped with that thing in the silence that will never end . . .

Then I really woke up.

The ice-cream vendor is cycling past my window, and the sparrows are squabbling over the crumbs I've put out for them on the sill. Those sparrows have helped me more than anything. The sparrows, and my little patch of garden, and watching the herons by the Serpentine. McLellan had the right idea when he kept Cedric. I'd like to think that one day, I too could have a dog. It would be company. Provided it wasn't scared.

Perhaps that's why Charles Tennant kept those spaniels. I've been thinking a lot about him lately. Poor bitter, guilty old man. And I understand a little better now how it was for him, because it's been much the same for me.

Every night, do you understand, I see them: that thing standing on the edge, and Kits trudging doggedly towards it.

Yes. I shall always see them.

Author's Note and Acknowledgements

Like Stephen, my first sight of Kangchenjunga came as a shock. I was staying in Darjeeling, and the previous day, I'd risen at 3.30a.m. and gone to the vantage point on Tiger Hill, hoping to glimpse the mountain at dawn — only to see nothing but cloud. The following morning, I drew back the curtains of my hotel room and there it was: vast, achingly clear, filling my window. Kangchenjunga had chosen its own time to reveal itself.

That was in April 2014, when as part of my research for *Thin Air*, I trekked with a small group of doughty hikers and even doughtier porters and dzos (a cross between a yak and a cow) into the foothills around Kangchenjunga. We followed the same route that Frank Smythe and G. O. Dyhrenfurth had taken in April 1930, and which the Cotterell expedition would take in the story: driving from Darjeeling to the Sikkimese village of Yuksom, then climbing on foot through the jungle to the uplands of Dzongri. We camped at Dzongri for some days and explored the surrounding region, hiking to a nearby pass and a sacred lake,

Lakshmi Pokari (official name Kabur Lam Lake); gaining startling views of Kangchenjunga; and experiencing, during one never-to-be-forgotten night, the most violent storm I've ever been in.

I made up the Lyell and Cotterell expeditions and everyone who took part in them, but all the other mountaineers mentioned in the story, such as Bauer, Smythe, and of course Mallory and Irvine, were real people who climbed in the Himalayas and/or attempted the summit of Kangchenjunga — sometimes paying with their lives, like Alexis Pache, whose grave lies at the foot of the mountain.

To evoke those times, I've retained many of the old-fashioned spellings. My characters' attitudes are also of the period, and this includes their racism, which one finds in many, although not all, contemporary accounts. (On that note, the "Crowley" mentioned in the story was the so-called "Aleister" Crowley, an unpleasant, self-aggrandizing fantasist who treated his porters appallingly.)

To create the Lyell and Cotterell expeditions, I've drawn on many of these early accounts, and I've been endlessly astonished by the toughness and bravery of the early climbers. Paul Bauer really did hack out large ice caves high on Kangchenjunga's north-west face; and his dog Wastl climbed with him to about twenty-four thousand feet. Nor did I invent that lady mountaineer friend of Aunt Ruth's. In the early 1900s an American named Fanny Bullock Workman unfurled a "Votes For Women" banner high in the Karakorams, and left her visiting card in a glass jar on one of the peaks.

The Cotterell expedition's route up the south-west face largely follows that of the British team led by Charles Evans, who were the first to reach the summit in 1955. However, in the interests of clarity, I've simplified both the route and the mountain's topography, omitting features not relevant to the story, such as the Hogsback and the Great Buttress, while keeping such major features as the Great Shelf, the Icefall and what I've called "the Buttress" (which is actually the Western Buttress).

In 1955 as in 1935, Kangchenjunga was a sacred mountain, and for many people it remains so today. It says a lot for its power that Charles Evans' party had to promise the Sikkimese government not to desecrate the summit by standing on the very top. They kept their word. When George Band and Joe Brown reached the summit on May 25th 1955, they resisted the urge to climb the last five feet; as did Norman Hardie and Tony Streather the following day. So did Major Prem Ghand and Naik Nima Dorje Sherpa of the Indian expedition in 1977; and Doug Scott, Peter Boardman and Joe Tasker, who reached the summit without oxygen in 1979 (at the time, one of them remarked that they didn't want to upset whatever lived up there). Kangchenjunga remained the "untrodden peak" until 1980, when a Japanese expedition stood on the top.

Concerning the history of climbing in the region, I'm particularly indebted to the following: *Climbing and Exploration in the Karakoram-Himalayas* (W. M. Conway, London 1894); *Climbing on the Himalaya and Other Mountain Ranges* (J. N. Collie, Edinburgh

1902); *Round Kangchenjunga* (D. W. Freshfield, London 1903); *Mountain Craft* (G. W. Young, 1920); *The Kangchenjunga Adventure* (F. S. Smythe, London 1930); *Kamet Conquered* (F. S. Smythe, London 1932); *The Naked Mountain* (E. Knowlton, New York 1933); *Annapurna* (M. Herzog, London 1952); *Kangchenjunga Challenge* (P. Bauer, London 1955); *Kanchenjunga* (J. Tucker, London 1955); *Kangchenjunga the Untrodden Peak* (C. Evans, London 1956); *The Boardman Tasker Omnibus* (P. Boardman & J. Tasker, London 1996); *Nanda Devi Exploration and Ascent* (E. Shipton & H. W. Tilman, compilation London 1999); *Fallen Giants: A History of Himalayan Mountaineering from the Age of Empire to the Age of Extremes* (M. Isserman & S. Weaver, Yale 2008).

Concerning altitude sickness and psychiatry in the 1900s–30s, the following were especially useful: *High Life: A History of High-Altitude Physiology and Medicine* (J. West, New York: OUP 1998); *High Altitude, Illness and Wellness: the Prevention of a Killer* (C. S. Houston, Connecticut 1998); *Psychology and Psychotherapy* (W. Brown, London 1934); *Instinct and the Unconscious* (W. H. Rivers, London 1922).

I'm also very grateful to Jan Faull and Rob Turnock for staging the British Film Institute's "Extreme Summits" season at the National Film Theatre in autumn 2013. It was an immense stroke of luck to be able to watch the original films of those early Himalayan expeditions on the big screen, particularly: John Noel's 1922 and 1924 films of the Everest climbs, Frank Smythe's 1931 film of his ascent of Kamet;

Wings over Everest (1934) directed by Ivor Montagu and Geoffery Barkas; and Charles Evans' footage of the 1955 ascent, which was given its first ever public screening at the NFT.

Finally, I want to thank a few people. First, Nawang Ldorba Leh of World Expeditions (India). Nawang was the Chief Guide on my trek to Dzongri. He has over twenty years' experience of trekking and climbing in Sikkim, Himachal, Ladakh and elsewhere, and I'm truly grateful for his expertise, his good humour and patience with my endless questions, and his kindness in taking me to that sacred lake. My thanks also to Om Bhadhur Chattri ("Jatha"), who has over the years made that Yuksom to Dzongri trek over two hundred and fifty times, and who was tireless on our trek in showing us the plants and wildlife of this very special region.

I also want to thank Jon Wood, Group Publisher, Orion Publishing Group, for his boundless enthusiasm for this project and his insightful editorial comments; as well as Jemima Forrester, Senior Commissioning Editor, and Bethan Jones, Assistant Editor, for their helpful and imaginative suggestions during the editing. Finally, my thanks as always to my wonderful agent Peter Cox, for his unfailing support for this story, from its very first glimmerings in the winter of 2012.

MICHELLE PAVER,
London 2015

DARK MATTER

Michelle Paver

January, 1937. Twenty-eight-year-old Jack is poor, lonely and desperate to change his life. So when he's offered the chance to be the wireless operator on an Arctic expedition, he jumps at it.

Five men and eight huskies, cross the Barents Sea from Norway by the light of the midnight sun. At last they reach the remote, uninhabited bay where they will camp. Gruhuken. But the Arctic summer is brief. As night returns to claim the land, Jack feels a creeping unease. One by one, his companions are forced to leave. He has to decide, stay or go.

Soon he will see the last of the sun, the point of no return — when the sea will freeze. And Gruhuken is not uninhabited. Something walks there in the dark.

THE SERPENT'S TOOTH

Michelle Paver

Since she was twelve years old, Belle has lived with a secret — a secret that cuts her off from her family and isolates her wherever she goes. Against the unfolding horror of the Great War, her search for peace takes her from the brittle gaiety of English country house society to the remote Scottish mansions where her grandmother's tragedy was played out, and to the battlefields of Flanders. As the scarred and shattered men return from the trenches, and the influenza epidemic scythes across the country, Belle must finally discover a way to break free of her secret — or lose her last chance of happiness.

FEVER HILL

Michelle Paver

For three years she had dreamed of coming back . . . In the summer of 1903, Sophie Munroe finally returns to her childhood home in Jamaica. Eden, the hauntingly beautiful plantation is nearly bankrupt and her sister Madeleine is hiding something. What can be so wrong that she cannot tell Sophie? Furthermore, her own inheritance, the house at Fever Hill, is slipping into ruin. There seems to be no-one to turn to and Sophie finds herself facing the savage prejudices of a colonial society and the need to confront the ghosts of her past . . .

THE SHADOW CATCHER

Michelle Paver

A spellbinding novel about families, secrets and dreams, the first in a trilogy about the Daughters of Eden. In the depths of the lush Jamaican forest stands a ruined house of haunting beauty, the last remains of a great estate founded on slavery. Abandoned for decades, it still casts its spell down the generations. A place of dreams, magic and madness. Worlds away, ten-year-old Madeleine's untroubled Scottish childhood is cut short after a fateful encounter with the handsome but hostile Cameron Lawe. Left alone to raise her newborn sister, Sophie, she seizes her chance to escape and returns to the decaying Jamaican plantation where she was conceived. There she finds a people haunted by a savage legacy and a family torn apart by obsession and betrayal. But there, too, she finds Eden, where she must finally confront the shadows of her own past.

THIN AIR

The Himalaya— ... 1935. Five English ... off f...
Darjeeling, d... ...
the summit ...
on earth. Th...
Lyell, leader ...
years before, ...
of extreme od...
far — and t...
Charles Tenn...
haunted by ...
things ahead ...
events hint th...
or safe — as ...
the horrors ...
refuses to sta...
won't set you ...